Also by Pat Garwood

Keyne Island

Walnuts

Best Way Out

Through a Crack in the Door

Pat Garwood

For Manny

Chapter One

The child saw it all.

Through a crack in the door he saw his father holding the woman round her neck. He was red in the face and bending her back over the table and shouting at her.

The woman was making a strange noise and the child saw her reach behind her and grab a knife off the table. She twisted round and pushed it hard into his father's stomach. His father let out a loud roar and staggered back from her. The child ran upstairs and hid under the covers in his bedroom.

He knew that roar and waited, shaking, for footsteps coming heavily up the stairs and the smacking that would follow. He knew he was in trouble. He shouldn't have been out of bed. He shouldn't have watched. He was a bad boy.

There was silence.

Then more noises. A shout, a groan, a loud thump.

Silence.

Then he heard someone coming up the stairs. There was a slight creak as his door was pushed open. He kept really still and pretended to be asleep.

After a moment or two, the child heard the person go back downstairs and then the sound of the front door slamming shut.

He got up and peeped through the curtains. It was quite dark but he saw the woman get in a car and drive away.

He was on his own with Daddy.

He was too frightened to go downstairs. He quickly got back into bed.

He would stay there until Mummy came back.

§

When the child woke in the morning, he found himself curled up in his bed with Mummy, who was still dressed.

'Morning Georgie,' she said giving him a kiss and smoothing his hair back from his face. She looked as if she had been crying.

He looked beyond her and round the room, anxiously.

'Where's Daddy?' he asked.

She took his hand.

'Listen Darling,' she said, 'something bad happened to Daddy last night, and it means he's had to go away for a long time and that he won't ever be coming back to us.'

'Does that mean that he can't hurt us any more?' asked George solemnly.

Her eyes filled with tears.

'Yes, no more hurting, all right?'

'Alright, Mummy,' he said, touching the funny hard bandage on her wrist.

He wondered if he should tell her about the woman, but he didn't want to talk about it. It was horrid, and he didn't want Mummy to cry. He didn't like it when she cried. So he kept quiet.

'Now, come on, let's get you dressed. And guess what? We're going to stay a few nights with Nana and Grandad!'

His face lit up.

'Can we play with the dogs, like last time?' he asked.

'Of course we can,' said Mummy, 'but first, there are two nice men in the kitchen who want to have a quick chat with you, before we go.'

When they got downstairs, the sitting room door was shut and there were strange voices coming from inside.

'Who's in there, Mummy?' George asked.

'Just some cleaners, darling,' his mother said, taking hold of his hand, 'come on, let's go into the kitchen.'

The two detectives were standing by the sink.

'Well, hello young man,' said one of them to George, kneeling down in front of him, 'you're looking smart today, are you off somewhere?'

'We're going to see Nana and Grandad.'

'Good for you,' the detective went on, offering him a biscuit, 'did you sleep well, last night?'

George looked at his mother, who gave him an encouraging nod.

'Yes,' he answered, taking the biscuit. It was a custard cream, his favourite, and he was really hungry, 'I went to sleep straight away and when I woke up Mummy was in bed with me.'

'Was she indeed,' said the detective, smiling at him, 'and how old are you?'

'Five and a half,' said George.

'Well done,' said the detective, 'was it noisy downstairs when you were trying to get to sleep?' he went on casually, eating a biscuit himself.

The child had a sudden image of the woman and the knife going into Daddy. He shouldn't have seen it. He should have been in bed. He'd been a bad boy.

'No,' he lied, 'Daddy put me to bed and I didn't get up.'

'Good lad,' said the detective, 'and where was Mummy?'

'Mummy had to go to A&B because she hurt her hand.'

'A&E,' said his mother, gently.

'We know what he means,' said the man with a smile.

'How did you manage to do that, anyway?' said the other detective to George's mother, looking at her arm, which was in a sling with the plaster cast showing.

'Oh I slipped on some water on the bathroom floor and cracked my wrist on the edge of the bath,' she said.

'Nasty,' he replied.

George looked at her. He was about to say, 'Daddy pushed her', but the main detective ruffled his hair.

'That's all for now,' he said, 'off you go and have a good time with your Nana and Grandad.'

As they went through the hall, George noticed three small drops of red on the carpet. He wondered if Mummy had noticed too.

§

Nana and Grandad were waiting outside by their car to pick them up and they both gave the child a hug.

'Does he know what's happened?' Nana whispered to Rachael, as Grandad helped George into the back seat.

'Not really,' she answered, 'but he does know that Michael won't be coming back.'

'Oh my Lord, what a terrible business,' her mother said.

She'd never much cared for Michael as a son-in-law but she would never have wanted him murdered.

'Who on earth could have done it?' she said, looking pale and drawn.

As they drove off, she looked round at George in the back of the car, and gave him a smile.

'Alright, my special boy?' she asked him.

'Yes Nana,' he said snuggling in to his mother and sucking his thumb.

I thought he'd grown out of that, thought Nana.

§

At her parent's house, Rachael sat on the bed that she'd had as a teenager. George was downstairs with her mother who was making pancakes for him.

She was in a complete state of shock.

Who could possibly have wanted to kill Michael?

She found herself emotionally disconnected from what had happened the night before. She wouldn't allow herself to feel relief but it was in her mind somewhere, despite the horror of it all.

Her marriage had become a nightmare since Michael started to abuse her, over the last few years. It was as if he was jealous of George and the time she devoted to him, and wanted to make her pay for loving the child more than she loved him.

She couldn't tell her parents, her friends, or her sister. God knows what Michael would have done to her if she had. Slowly it had begun to sap her confidence, she lost weight and started looking scrawny, which he would often comment on.

She'd always managed to hide the cuts and bruises when he attacked her. He never touched her face, apart from slapping her, which left marks that were gone by the next day. It frequently happened in the evening after he'd had a few drinks but he could also suddenly turn on her at any odd moment of the day. It made her very nervous and jumpy. She was always walking on egg shells so as not to set him off.

Recently he'd started to punish George, if he thought he had been 'a bad boy'. Telling him off too strongly, and sometimes shutting him in his room or smacking him on the back of his legs. Usually for no good reason.

It broke her heart – she couldn't bear it. She'd been trying to find the courage to take George and go to a refuge or something.

And now this.

Michael was dead. It was over.

It had been horrendous, finding Michael collapsed in a sea of blood when she got back from the hospital. He seemed to have been stabbed in his stomach and chest and both his wrists were slashed. He was completely still and she knew instinctively that he was dead. She ran upstairs in a blind panic to see if George was alright. Mercifully he was sound asleep and breathing peacefully. She closed his door and went quickly downstairs and phoned the police. They arrived about twenty minutes later and so did a doctor. While she was waiting, she'd sat in the kitchen, resting her plaster cast on the table and staring at nothing. She was in a complete state of shock, unable to collect her thoughts.

It made no sense. He'd been murdered. Who could have done it? Why? Nothing in the room was disturbed. The remains of some supper were still on the table with a bottle of red wine, half drunk, and a glass which had been knocked over, but that was all. She'd been gone for about six hours, she reckoned.

A&E was incredibly busy and she'd had to wait ages to be seen, x-rayed, and have her wrist put in plaster.

Later on today, she had to go to the police station to talk further with the detectives. They were aware that she'd been at the hospital all evening so there was no fear of her being under suspicion. She'd tried to phone Michael several times during the evening, to check that George had gone to bed alright and to say it looked as if she was going to be there for some time, but he hadn't picked up, either on the home phone or his mobile. She'd left a message each time.

As she sat on her old bed, she waited for a huge sense of loss and grief to overwhelm her.

There was nothing.

She didn't realise until that moment that she had grown to hate him.

Chapter Two

The woman shut the door of the hotel room behind her and sank to the floor. She was trembling all over and felt violently sick.

She couldn't believe what had happened. She'd totally lost it.

She slowly got up and carried her handbag into the bathroom. She took the knife, wrapped in a bloody napkin, out of the bag. She must destroy all evidence, she thought as she dropped it into the basin. She turned on the tap and watched as the water turned red and the napkin unfolded. She lifted out the knife and ran it under the tap until it was shiny clean. She placed it carefully on the basin surround and rinsed the napkin until the water ran clear, but it was still heavily stained. She wrung it out and placed it next to the knife.

She looked at herself in the mirror. Who was that woman staring back at her, who had stabbed a man, not once but twice, then slashed his wrists and left him for dead?

She should go to the police at once and confess what she had done.

No, she was damned if she would. He had deserved it. A reptile. A destroyer of human sanity, human dignity.

She washed her hands over and over with soap, then ran a shower.

When she took off her clothes she could see that she had blood on her blouse and some on her skirt. She must get rid of it as quickly as possible. She filled the basin and put them to soak in cold water.

As she stood under the shower, letting it run over her, she was aware of a painful tenderness at the back of her head, where he'd banged it on the table, also she had a terrible ache in her throat where he'd tried to strangle her. She was seething with shock and anger. None of this was meant to happen. This was not the plan.

There was no way she could get arrested for this. She was needed to look after Kate. She couldn't spend time in prison.

Self-defence turned murder. Shit.

Of course her fingerprints would be found in the house, but she had never actually been in trouble with the law and they weren't on any data base. She'd never got caught for anything, she was too smart. As long as she kept a low profile and didn't get taken to a police station for any reason, how could they ever be traced back to her.

When she got home, she would take her stained clothes and the napkin, in a plastic bag, to the local recycling centre and toss it onto the huge pile of unwanted rubbish. The knife could be thrown over the 'metal only' section, never to be seen again.

She finally got herself into bed but she couldn't sleep. She kept going over and over what had happened.

§

'Be quiet, you stupid bitch, you'll wake the child,' he'd said as she cried out, when he hit her. He grabbed hold of her hair and banged her head hard on the dining table, three times.

'If you try anything like this again I swear to God I'll kill you,' he said, leaning over her and putting his hands round her throat.

Jesus Christ, he's going to strangle me, she thought, finding it hard to breathe with the pressure on her throat. He was losing control, she could see it in his face which was contorted with anger. He was twisting her to the right and her hand landed on the surface behind her, straight onto a knife. Without thinking twice she grabbed it, brought it round and plunged it into his stomach. He let out a roar, letting go of her throat and staggering backwards. As he did so, the knife came out of him and stayed gripped in her hand. With another roar he came for her again and she plunged the knife into his chest. It went right in up to the handle and he fell back with a crash cracking his head on the wooden floor as he went down, with his arms outstretched and the knife still in his chest. After a moment of shock when the world stood still, a red mist descended on her. She felt no fear now, she was just full of anger for the pain and damage that her Kate had suffered. Using all her strength, she bent down and pulled the knife out of him, then stood over him and slashed one of his wrists and then the other.

'That's for what you've done, you bastard.' she said.

He lay completely still. He looked dead.

She waited, frozen, for a minute. Half prepared for him to jump up suddenly and start attacking her again.

Slowly her breathing calmed down and she came to her senses.

Oh God, the child!

She quickly wrapped the knife in a napkin off the table and threw it into her bag then ran upstairs in case the child had heard everything. Thank God the boy seemed to be fast asleep. She checked next door in the bigger bedroom and then in a small box room but they were both empty. She hurried downstairs taking one last glance at the heavily bleeding man. He did look dead. But was he? She couldn't wait to find out, she had to get away. Now, at once. She grabbed her bag and coat, let herself out of the front door and ran to the car.

Running from the scene of the crime. 'Stab, slash and run', she thought grimly to herself as she drove back to her hotel. She understood why people fled after hitting someone with their car. It was too scary to face the consequences. A sense of survival took over. Save yourself from an unbearable situation. Get away as fast as you can. It was second nature, not reason, that took the upper hand.

Was he dead? She needed to be certain.

She would have to go back and find out.

Chapter Three

The child had wet the bed.

'Sorry Mummy', he said, 'will Daddy be cross with…….'

His words faded away as he remembered that Daddy wouldn't be angry because he was never coming back.

'It's alright, sweetheart,' Rachael said, giving him a kiss, 'it doesn't matter.'

He hadn't done that for a couple of years, she thought. He must be picking up on all the tension and tears going on around him. Thank God he'd slept through it all and knew nothing of what had happened.

She bundled up his sheets as best she could, the plaster cast making it really awkward. Then she put a towel over the mattress, where there was a big damp patch and pulled the coverlet over the top so it didn't look too messy. She'd come back later and sort it out with her Mum; they needed to find a plastic sheet if they were to stay for a few days.

She managed to get him out of his wet pyjamas and took him to the bathroom down the hall.

'Quick wash,' she said, soaping his bottom half with a flannel, careful not to get water on her cast.

'It's cold,' he squawked, wriggling from her.

'Come on Georgie,' she said wiping the soap off and towelling him dry with her right hand, 'you don't want to be smelly for Nana and Grandad.'

'Torvill and Dean are smelly, and they don't mind them,' he answered.

'Yes, well they're dogs, darling, that's different,' she said, smiling in spite of herself.

As if on cue, the two cocker spaniels pushed open the door and started rushing around the bathroom. Dean got hold of the wet flannel and rushed out of the room with it, Torvill raced after him and they had a tussling match on the landing, each trying to have it for his own.

George burst out laughing. It was a comfort for Rachael to hear it.

She had been feeling sick ever since she'd woken up and had to face the horrendous thing that had happened.

Michael had been murdered. In their own home.

It still didn't feel real and she was scared. Who had killed him? Might he come back and kill her and maybe even George? Was it a random killing or was it someone who Michael had crossed in a business deal? Was it a jealous husband? She had always had her suspicions about whether Michael had cheated on her but she had never dared broach it with him.

She brought her thoughts back to George.

'Right, let's get you dressed and go down and have some breakfast,' she said.

'Can we stay here tonight as well?' George said, 'I don't want to go home.'

Rachael looked at him, sharply. Did he know something?

'Why don't you?' she asked.

'It's nice here,' he said, running out into the hall.

He seemed OK. She wondered if it would be best for him to go to school today as usual. She couldn't drive because of her wretched wrist, but her mother would take him, she was sure. Luckily her parents only lived about fifteen minutes away from his school.

Her head was swimming. There was so much to think about. What would all this mean for her and George? Would they still be able to live in their house? Would she want to? Where on earth could they go if they didn't go home? She knew it would be too much for her parents if she and George stayed with them for more than a week or so.

The house was in both her and Michael's names, thank goodness, otherwise she could have been in real trouble. Even so, she would be responsible for paying the mortgage now, wouldn't she? How was she going to do that? And did he have Life Insurance? She didn't know. Even if he had, it would be months before the estate would be settled.

She had no idea how much money Michael had. They had a joint current account, which at first she thought was very generous of him. Until she discovered that he would grill her once a month about any money she had paid out, so she felt she was forever on the bread-line and worried about having spent too much. Of course he had other savings accounts, she knew, but what was in them she had no idea. And did he have any debts that she didn't know about? Would she be responsible for them?

At breakfast it was decided that her father would go with her to the police station, and her mother would stay home with George. It wouldn't hurt him to miss a couple of days school, and he might get a sudden reaction to his father's disappearance.

§

Rachael felt very shaky being interviewed by the police. They asked so many questions about her and Michael. Who were his friends? Did he have any enemies? Who did they see socially? Were they happy together? Had they received any strange phone calls recently?

They explained that they had taken away his computer, lap-top and mobile, to search for any clues into what had happened. They promised to keep her informed of any developments. As with all violent deaths, there would have to be a post-mortem investigation, they told her, which would be followed at a later date by an inquest, once the police had gathered evidence and had found any witnesses. When the results of the post-mortem were known, the coroner would be able to release the body for burial or cremation. A death certificate couldn't be issued until after the inquest but a temporary one could be given, in order to settle the estate and deal with some of the financial issues.

They would let her know when she was able to move back into her home. Probably within a week, once the police had finished any tests in the house and garden, that might provide evidence.

Did she have any questions?

Rachael burst into tears. It was all too much. They passed over tissues and handed her a glass of water. The policewoman who had been sitting in the interview room with them got up and put her hand on her shoulder.

'Poor thing,' she said sympathetically, 'a terrible shock for you to lose someone you love, in such horrific circumstances.'

What about the shock of losing someone you *didn't* love, Rachael thought, as the tears fell. She felt so guilty, not to be feeling any real grief. But all the pain she'd felt over the last few years, not just physically but from all the broken dreams, rose to the surface. She had loved him so much at the beginning but that memory was ruined forever by what came after.

'I think that's all for now,' said the detective, 'you have your father outside to take you back to your parents' house, is that right?'

She nodded dumbly, wiping the flow of tears.

Oh God, there'd have to be a funeral. She didn't think she could go through with it. All the condolences. All the pretence.

'Keep strong,' the detective said patting her on the arm as he showed her out, 'we'll do everything we can to find his killer.'

'Thank you,' she mumbled, and made her way to where her father was sitting on a hard chair, waiting for her. He looked sad and so old, she suddenly thought. When had that happened?

§

When they got back to her parents house, she found George in the kitchen with her mother. They'd got the crayons out and were doing some drawing.

'He's been such a good boy,' her mother said, 'oh, you look worn out. I'll make you a cup of tea,' she got up and went to switch the kettle on.

Rachael went round behind George and looked over his shoulder at his picture.

He'd drawn a picture of a rainbow on one side of the paper and a black cloud on the other. Under the rainbow were two stick people, with smiley faces.

'That's you and me,' said George, pointing at them.

'And who are these two?' Rachael said pointing to the two stick people drawn under the big black cloud. Their faces were roughly scratched in, with red.

'That's Daddy and the lady,' he said.

Chapter Four

The woman woke with a start. She was pouring with sweat and gasping for breath. He had been trying to strangle her and push her down into the mud. Her head was slowly going under and she could feel the mud getting into her ears and nose. She opened her mouth to scream and it filled with the slimy dark mud, choking her. She was going to die. She made one last super-human attempt to throw him off her and woke herself up. She was sitting bolt upright in bed, the bedclothes tangled around her and nothing but the darkness of the room and her own heavy breathing.

She took a minute or two to remember where she was, why she was there and what she had done. She looked at the clock: 3 a.m. She got up and went to the window, pulling aside the hotel blackout curtain and the flimsy net behind it. She managed to open the sliding window about three inches before its safety lock prevented it going any further. Great in a fire, she thought ironically as she pressed her face to the gap and drank in the cool night air. She took a few deep breaths and closed it again, pulled the curtains shut and stumbled back to turn on the bedside light.

It was so bright it hurt her eyes. She sat on the side of the bed and tried to think clearly. The plan had gone horribly wrong and she was now in deep trouble. It was never meant to end like this.

Initially it had been mind-blowing just to finally find out where he lived and she had decided to go and suss out what sort of house he lived in, the bastard. She'd booked into a cheap hotel for the night, in case she needed to do something under the cover of darkness. Maybe she'd post something through the letter box or ring the bell and see who answered. Maybe even go in and confront him.

He'd made the mistake of being interviewed on television in his road, when he was complaining with neighbours about the council cutting down an elm tree on the wide pavement. He'd said he lived at number 6.

'That's him!' Kate had said, watching the evening news, 'Mum, that's the man. That's his voice. He's the one,' she put her hand up to her mouth and started shaking all over, 'oh, I'm going to be sick,' she'd said as she bent over in her wheelchair and spewed up all over her knees and slippers.

The woman hated him on sight. He looked like a smug politician.

§

When she had arrived at his road, it was just beginning to get dark. She parked the car on the other side from number 6 and stared at the house. Posh, she thought. He had money. The front garden was well cared for and there was some kind of blue plaque on the wall.

As she was looking, a taxi drew up and a woman came out of the front door of the house clutching her left wrist, obviously in pain. It figured. She got in the taxi and it pulled out and drove off. She saw a fleeting glimpse of a man looking out of a top window. It was him!

It was too good a chance to miss. She got out of her car, made sure she had the photos in her bag, just in case, and crossed the road.

She was nervous and very angry. Seeing him like that in his smart home brought all the suffering of the last ten years to the surface and gave her the courage to go ahead with the plan.

She went up the five steps to the front door. Lifted the brass knocker, in the shape of a lion, and rapped on the door, hard, three times.

After a minute or two - he opened the door.

Chapter Five

'That's Daddy and that's the lady.'

Uh uh, here comes trouble, thought Grandad, peering down at the picture.

'Come on, George,' he said, 'let's go and play ball in the garden.'

The child followed him and so did the dogs, leaving behind a shocked Rachael and her mother, staring at the drawing that he'd left on the kitchen table.

'Oh Darling, I'm so sorry,' her mother said, 'who do you think she is?'

'I don't know Mum,' said Rachael, 'maybe he's just making something up.'

'I don't think so,' said her mother, grimly.

'Do you think we should show it to the police?' Rachael asked, 'whoever she is, she might have something to do with Michael being killed.'

'Let's talk to George a bit more about it,' said her mother cautiously, 'he might tell us something that he wouldn't say to strangers. We can always phone the police tomorrow.'

'I guess so,' said Rachael looking at the drawing, distractedly. 'Do you think Michael was having an affair?' her mother asked.

'Oh God, I don't know, Mum. It's possible,' said Rachael.

The bastard, thought her mother. She took Rachael in her arms and gave her a hug, 'I'm so sorry you're having to go through all this,' she said.

Rachael felt tears sliding down her face and landing on her mother's blue jumper. She was comforted by the familiar warmth of the embrace. It had been so long since Michael had held her with tenderness and love. Any form of touching had only led to one of two things. Sex, whether she wanted it or not, or pain inflicted on some part of her body.

Her mother knew a thing or two about being cheated on, although she had never discussed it with Rachael or her sister. It had happened a couple of times during her marriage. Her husband had no idea that she suspected him, but of course she knew. So many small indications and changes in his behaviour. It had made her deeply unhappy but she'd decided to say nothing for the sake of the children. And as each affair blew itself out, life returned to normal and they continued on, in what was otherwise a happy marriage.

In the garden, Grandad and the child sat on the bench, getting their breath back and watching Torvill and Dean race round the apple tree.

'So what was that picture all about, Georgie,' he asked. Straight in there.

'What picture?' said George, throwing a tennis ball a short way up in the air and catching it.

'You, know - you and Mummy, and Daddy and the lady.'

'Daddy's never coming back,' said George.

'Is that so?' said Grandad carefully.

'Yes, Mummy said.'

'Ah,' Grandad paused for a bit and then went on in an even tone, 'and who was the lady?'

'What lady?' said George, throwing the ball up again.

'The lady in the picture.'

'I don't know,' said George.

'But there was a lady?' asked Grandad, after a pause.

'Where?' said George.

'With Daddy?'

'Yes. But don't tell Mummy, or you'll make her cry,' said George throwing the ball for the dogs who went chasing after it.

'Right,' said Grandad, rubbing his hand across his face.

He had suspected that there might be some sort of marital problem at the heart of the tragedy. Maybe Michael had been having an affair with 'the lady' and the murder was an act of revenge on the part of her husband. He knew from his own experience how tangled life became if you strayed off the straight and narrow. It had happened to him a couple of times during his 45 years of marriage. Nothing serious, but there had been a few hairy moments which had made him realise how much was at stake and what a fool he was being. Fortunately his wife never had a clue what was going on, she would have been devastated and probably thrown him out.

Or perhaps Michael had got into debt and borrowed money from the wrong sort of people. He would be surprised, though, if that were the case because he had been a bright guy and seemed to know what he was about. They'd actually got on quite well, they both liked cricket, which helped. Not that they'd seen him that much as he was often too busy working.

'Can we stay with you for ever, Grandad?' George piped up, breaking into his thoughts.

What a question. They loved having Rachael and George over for an afternoon but it was usually quite exhausting. There was always a sense of relief when peace returned and they could settle down to a quiet evening watching television.

'Oh, we'll see what happens, don't you worry about it. We'll have lots of fun while you're here, won't we,' he said, roughing up George's hair, jokily.

'Yes, we will,' said George, jumping off the bench, 'can we kick the ball around again, Grandad?'

'I think that's enough for me,' said Grandad, putting his hand up to his chest and giving it a rub.

'Well, can we have a look in your shed, then?' asked George.

'Oh, alright,' Grandad said, smiling and easing himself up off the bench.

George loved Grandad's shed. It was full of so many different and extraordinary old things. It had a special rusty oily smell.

Grandad opened the latch and they went in. George stood on an old box and looked over at a shelf. There were tins of nails and screws and another one full of rusty old keys.

'What are these for?' he asked.

'I've no idea,' laughed Grandad, 'I just keep them because I like all the different shapes. I used to have them up on a board hanging on hooks, but when we moved here they ended up in that tin!'

'What's this,' asked George, picking up a dark red shiny handle.

'Oh, that's my old pocket knife,' said Grandad taking it from him, 'that went everywhere with me when I was a young man.'

He pulled at one end and it opened out into a thin silver blade.

'Wow,' said George, staring at it.

'Have to be careful with that, it's really sharp,' said Grandad, snapping it closed and putting it back on the shelf.

'Come on,' he said to George, 'let's go in and have some tea.'

He started back out of the shed and George quickly nipped back onto the box, reached for the knife and slipped it into his pocket.

If the lady came back to kill Mummy he could use it to stab her and make her leave Mummy alone.

'Coming Grandad,' he said, and they went back up the path, holding hands.

When they got into the kitchen, Nana and Mummy had laid out some Marmite sandwiches, a few bourbon biscuits and a sponge cake with jam in the middle.

'It's not much, but it'll keep us going till supper,' Nana said.

Mum looks really tired, thought Rachael as she looked across the table at her. Well, it had been a massive shock for all of them. Except George bless him, who thankfully had no idea about what happened.

George saw Nana push a knife into the centre of the cake, and watched the jam oozing out, as she cut a slice.

'I don't want any tea,' he said suddenly and ran out of the kitchen, up the stairs and onto his bed. He took out the pocket knife and managed to open it. It was a bit stiff but he did it. He looked at the thin silver blade and then plunged it into his pillow. Yes, he thought, that's how he'd do it.

It felt good.

Chapter Six

Next morning, the woman went into the hotel bathroom and wrung out her blouse and skirt. The vibrant red of the blood had faded but they were still noticeably stained. She balled them up and put them in a plastic bag she'd brought with her, that she'd had snacks and juices in. She hadn't wanted to visit any restaurants while she was here; a low profile was the order of the day. Luckily she'd got her black trousers with her and a black hooded sweatshirt in case it got colder. So she put those on and stared at herself in the mirror.

How can you blackmail a dead man? You can't. That was the answer.

Was he dead? He must be, surely.

She had to be certain.

She turned on the television and had to wait for about twenty minutes of mindless drivel before the news.

There'd been another earthquake in Italy. Eighty people known to have died.

What difference does one more body make, she thought. People are dying right now all over the world. It's the living who are important. Like her Kate and the woman and child he'd left behind. If he was dead.

A panda had a new baby.

Another railway strike affecting hundreds of passengers. People having their lives messed up again. Losing jobs, money, marriages.

Then it came.

'The director of 'Out There Health Clubs' was murdered in his own home at approximately 8.30 p.m. last night. The police are appealing for anyone who thinks they may have information concerning his death or who saw anything unusual near the scene of the crime, to come forward and assist with their enquiries.'

There was a picture of his house with yellow and black tape cordoning it off. The report was being given on the pavement by a presenter with blonde hair and too much make up. In the background men in white paper overalls could be seen taking equipment into the house.

She'd done it!

He was dead!

She was appalled by what she'd done, but glad that he was no longer around to rape any more women.

She didn't need to go back to the house today, not now she knew. She must go home, back to her daughter.

Kate must never know what she'd done. No-one must ever know, it was the only way. She must go back to living a normal life – alternative mission accomplished.

'He leaves behind his wife and their five-year-old son,' the presenter went on in a sombre tone, as the television brought up a picture of the man's wife and son, happy on a beach with the sun and sea behind them.

'Five years old. Bloody hell!' the woman said. Hopefully the mother had returned before he came downstairs and saw what had happened. He had looked fast asleep when she peered into his room. What effect would it have on him to lose his father in such a horrific way, and what about his wife, the pretty smiling brunette shown on the screen. Where would life take her now? Maybe to greener grass. She hoped so, poor cow.

She switched off the television, turned on her mobile and phoned home.

Kate picked up at once.

'Mum, thank God you've phoned. Have you seen the news? He's dead, someone's killed him! I can't believe it. Did you get to see him before it happened?'

'I've just seen it on the television, Kate,' she answered in a shocked tone, 'No, I didn't see him. I went to the house earlier in the afternoon but there was no-one in,' she lied, 'I thought I might try again today, but now this has happened I won't be able to, of course. So I never had the chance to put our plan into action.'

'So he hasn't seen the photos?' Kate asked.

'No. We've missed the moment I'm afraid.'

'Damn,' said Kate, 'well anyway, he's got what he deserved. Who do you think did it?'

'Probably some man who had a grievance with him,' said her mother, trying to put her off the scent.

'Maybe it was just a violent robbery,' said Kate.

'Look, don't let's talk about it any more,' said the woman, feeling sick as she remembered the horror of it all, 'how is everything going with you, did you manage to get yourself some breakfast? Could you manage OK with your crutches?'

'I'm fine. When are you coming home?'

'I'll be back by teatime,' the woman said, 'I think we should forget all about this now and try and move on with our lives.'

'Easy for you to say,' said Kate, grimly.

'No, it's not Kate, it's really not,' the woman said hotly.

'Alright Mum, calm down,' said Kate.

'I'll see you later,' the woman said and ended the call.

She sat in the small hard armchair and tried to think if there was anything that would lead the murder enquiry back to her.

There was the car, of course. If anyone had noticed it and taken a photo of the number plate, then she'd had it. But why would they?

She was not safely out of the woods by any means. She needed to have luck on her side if she was to get away with this. If she'd only stabbed him once, she could have pleaded self-defence, but not with the knife in his chest as well and the slashing of his wrists.

She couldn't face the thought of being arrested and kept in jail pending a court case. Especially since Kate was so dependent on her and they were so badly in debt.

She was going to have to think up a new plan.

Chapter Seven

'Were you aware that your husband was having an affair?' the Chief Inspector asked Rachael, who was sitting on the sofa, with her plaster cast resting on the arm.

The police had arrived at her parents' home, mid-morning, about three days after Michael had been killed. Her mother had driven George to his infant school for the first time since it had happened and was going on to the supermarket and her father had taken Torvill and Dean for a walk in the park, so Rachael was on her own.

'I'm sorry?' she said, shocked; unprepared for the question.

'Your husband. Were you aware that he was having an affair?'

'No, not really,' she said, feeling her face flushing.

'Not really? Does that mean you had your suspicions?'

'Well, yes, no, I don't know. I sometimes wondered if he was, but I was never sure,' she mumbled and then asked after a pause, 'who was he having an affair with?'

She almost didn't want to know. Supposing it was one of their friends, how awful that would be.

The next question turned her world upside down.

'Do you know anyone called Lorna,' he asked her, watching her intently.

The blood drained from her face.

There was only one person she knew called Lorna.

Her sister.

It couldn't be. He wouldn't, surely to God. Lorna wouldn't – would she?

She and Lorna had never been that close. The last time they had been together was at a family wedding about a year ago. She suddenly had a flash of watching Michael and Lorna dancing together at one point during the evening and being glad that they seemed to be getting on well. Lorna could be quite difficult, almost rude sometimes.

'Only my sister' she said, 'but I'm sure she would never…' she tailed off, unable to carry on.

'Well we'll check that out, obviously,' said the Chief Inspector, 'it may well turn out to be another woman entirely. We only have that name from her texts to him, on his pay as you go.'

'He doesn't have a pay as you go.'

'He did, I'm afraid, as did this 'Lorna', it appears he kept it only for contact with her.'

Her mind was racing ahead. She knew it was her sister. So many things began to fall into place. Lorna hardly ever answered her calls any more. Always so busy with her job. Michael was never interested in talking about her, to the point that she'd felt quite hurt. Oh God, her parents would be devastated if they found out.

'If it does turn out to be my sister,' she said, aware her breathing was all over the place, 'is it possible to keep this from my parents, it would really upset them.'

'I'm afraid these things have a habit of coming out during a murder enquiry. Let's just hope for your sake that it's not her,' he said.

'She's married,' said Rachael, thinking of Lorna's husband, Chris, a slightly boring estate agent.

'Often the way,' commented the Chief Inspector, dryly, 'but she has nothing to worry about if she's not the woman in question, however we will need to eliminate her from our enquiries. We'll be in contact with her in due course.'

This is going from bad to worse, thought Rachael, frantically. If it was Lorna, would Chris have had the balls to murder Michael, if he found out about the affair? Who knows? The mildest people can suddenly turn, if they're pushed too far. You read it in the papers all the time.

'The forensic team have now finished with everything in the house and garden,' he said rising from the armchair, 'you're free to return to the property at any time you wish.'

'What about the blood stains?' whispered Rachael.

'I'm afraid it's the home owners responsibility to deal with the mess that's left in the house,' said the Detective Inspector who had been quiet throughout the interview, 'you might find this useful,' he said kindly, and handed her a list of crime scene cleaners, 'they are very efficient and are usually able to come quite quickly, and we also advise you to change the locks on the house – just as a precaution.'

'Thank you,' she said to him, gratefully. Maybe her parents would be able to help her arrange it all.

Perhaps she should go back to live in the house, once the bloodstains had been removed or covered up. It would probably be the best thing for George. After all he didn't know what had happened. He'd be in his own room with his Lego, his books and toys. And it would be quiet and peaceful without the threat of Michael's violence. But could she bear it? She felt as if the murder would somehow permeate through the rooms. She loved her parents very much but it felt all wrong to be living in their house again. It seemed such a backward step, negating all the progress she had made in her life since she'd left home. Perhaps she should put the house up for sale straight away and rent somewhere until it sold. Would she have the money to do that? Her thoughts were swirling around in her head.

'Just one last thing,' said the Chief Inspector, as they made their way to the door.

'Yes?'

'It has become apparent that your husband was murdered by a woman.'

Chapter Eight

Dear God, was it Lorna?

Had Lorna murdered Michael?

Had they been having an affair?

After the detectives had left, Rachael sank onto the sofa.

She hadn't seen or spoken to Lorna since Michael's death. Her mother had told her that she was really poorly with flu and couldn't get out of bed.

Rachael had received only one text from her saying 'so awful to hear the news about Michael, I'm devastated'.

I'll bet you are, thought Rachael, her mind spinning as she tried to get her head round everything that was happening.

Lorna and Michael having an affair? Was it possible? Did they have sex in her house? Had George seen them? Was Lorna 'the lady' in his drawing? Was Lorna the woman who killed Michael. Oh God, she needed to to calm down and think clearly. She mustn't jump to conclusions. Maybe it was another Lorna who he'd been having the affair with.

She had to find out quickly.

She got up and lifted the receiver of the house phone and pressed for Lorna. She answered at once.
'Mum?'

'No, it's me.'

'Oh... Rachael, are you alright? I'm so sorry I haven't phoned but I've been really ill. What an awful thing to have happened,' she started crying, 'I can't believe he's gone.'

'OK, listen to me,' Rachael cut in, 'where were you the night Michael was killed?'

'What? I was at the cinema with Chris, why?'

'Thank God.'

'What?'

'I'll explain later. Lorna, you have to leave the flat now, at once. We have to talk – it's urgent. I'll meet you by the pond, in the park at the end of Mum and Dad's road, in half an hour.'

'Oh, no I can't, Rachael, I'm sorry I'm too poorly,' she replied, sniffing and coughing.

'You have to come. The police have Michael's phone and all the texts he sent on it. You may be implicated. They want to talk to you and might arrive at your flat at any moment. You could be in big trouble. See you in half an hour. Be there.'

She put the phone down and wrote a note for her mother saying she had to go out and that she'd return before George was back from school. The phone rang and 'Lorna' came up on the display. She ignored it. She put the note on the kitchen table and left the house.

She got herself a take-away coffee en route, and took it into the park, then sat on one of the benches by the pond and waited for Lorna.

She would know at once, as soon as they met, if it was true about the affair. She'd always been able to tell if Lorna was lying. She was three years older than her and it was a tricky relationship at the best of times. As an adult, Lorna had revealed a pretty dodgy moral code, but she would never have thought she could stoop so low as to have an affair with her own sister's husband.

When Lorna arrived, ten minutes later, she looked terrible. She was red-faced, her eyelids were swollen, she was crying and she looked scared.

'Is it true?' Rachael asked her straight away, 'were you having an affair with Michael?'

Lorna's face crumpled, 'I'm so sorry, Rachael,' she said, not even trying to deny it, 'I never wanted it to happen but he went on and on trying, and eventually I just gave in. I didn't know what to do.'

'How could you?' said Rachael, standing to face her, 'it's the worst thing you could have done to me.'

'I know, I know, I'm so sorry, do you think you'll ever be able to forgive me?'

'I doubt it,' said Rachael, getting a deep, aching pain in her chest, as bad as anything she'd ever experienced. Worse than Michael hitting her. She felt sick with the betrayal, both from Lorna and Michael, and sank down onto the bench again.

'I couldn't stop it or talk to anyone about it,' Lorna went on, sitting next to her, still crying, 'and I was so frightened that you would find out, or that Chris would. I've felt so guilty, it's been awful.'

'It must have been,' said Rachael, dryly.

'Please don't tell Chris or Mum and Dad,' Lorna said, 'they wouldn't understand, they'd just think I was a terrible person.'

'Yes,' said Rachael.

'You won't tell, will you?'

Rachael looked at her sister. She would never feel the same about her after this. It was almost like talking to a stranger.

'I think you've blown it Lorna. It's all going to come out and everyone will know. There's nothing we can do to stop it. The police have got Michael's phone with all your messages and texts to each other.'

'Oh my God,' said Lorna covering her face with her hands, 'I'm so sorry Rachael.'

'It's too late to be sorry,' said Rachael, 'Michael's dead.'

She suddenly got a flash of him lying there, stabbed, with his wrists slashed and blood all over the floor.

'Have the police got any idea about the man who killed him?' asked Lorna.

'Actually, they think it was a woman,' said Rachael, looking at her intently.

Lorna took a beat and then an intake of breath.

'They don't think *I* had anything to do with it, do they?'

'I don't know,' said Rachael, 'are you sure you were at the cinema that night, and were with Chris the whole time?'

'Yes of course, I'm sure,' a look of panic crossed Lorna's face, 'but if he finds out about me and Michael he'll be furious. He might even deny he was with me,' she started crying again.

'Yes, he might,' said Rachael fishing in her bag.

She knew Lorna so well. She was sure that she hadn't murdered Michael.

But she had slept with him.

'When did it start?' she said steadily, handing her a tissue.

'The day after Elizabeth's wedding,' said Lorna, blowing her nose, 'he turned up at the flat after Chris had gone off to work and made a massive move on me. I tried to say no but I couldn't stop him and it just went on from there,' she was still crying.

Neither of them spoke for a few seconds.

'Did he ever hurt you?' said Rachael. It was out before she could help it. She needed to know.

Lorna stopped crying and looked at Rachael, shocked.

'No. Why, did he hurt you?' she said looking at Rachael's plaster cast and then up at her face.

Rachael felt her throat seize up. She couldn't speak. She had never told anyone about what had happened.

She nodded briefly and then turned away.

'Oh my God, I'm so sorry,' Lorna said, putting her arm round her shoulder.

'Don't,' said Rachael, shaking her off.

'Why didn't you tell me?'

Rachael shrugged.

'Did it happen a lot?' Lorna asked.

Rachael nodded.

'Do Mum and Dad know?'
'No,' said Rachael, shaking her head.

'Did George ever see it happening?'

'Sometimes,' she said, 'I was planning to leave and go to a woman's refuge with him, and then this happened.'

'The bastard,' said Lorna, leaning back against the bench.

'Yeah,' said Rachael, shakily.

'Did you still love him?' asked Lorna.

'No, not by the end.'

'Why didn't you tell someone?'

'I couldn't,' said Rachael.

She'd become scared of what he might do to her if she told anyone. She'd already lost friends because he was jealous if she had any social life that didn't include him, and he'd always take it out on her when she returned.

'I feel so bad for you and I hate myself so much,' said Lorna, shrinking into the bench.

Rachael looked at her.

'Did *you* love Michael?' she asked.

'Not really,' said Lorna turning her tear-stained face to Rachael, 'I knew it was wrong. I just didn't know how to stop it.'

There was silence for a minute or two, as they both stared out over the water.

'Who could have killed him, who *is* she?' said Lorna, 'do you think he was having an affair with someone else as well?'

'I wouldn't put it past him,' said Rachael.

'No,' said Lorna, wiping her eyes and frowning, she had a cracking headache.

'Listen, don't tell the police about Michael attacking me,' said Rachael, 'they might think that I'm somehow involved in his death, which I'm not, by the way.'

'Of course not, I never thought you were,' said Lorna, 'Mum said you were at A&E all evening, anyway.'

'Mum and Dad think this was an accident,' said Rachael, holding up her plastered wrist, 'they didn't know what was happening and hopefully they never will, it would only upset them.'

'Unless George tells them,' said Lorna.

Rachael hesitated for a moment and then told Lorna about George's picture and 'the lady'.

'Bloody hell, Rachael, do you think he saw something? I mean 'the lady' couldn't have been me. We never did anything in your house, I wouldn't, it was only in my flat.'

'Oh good,' said Rachael dryly.

She suddenly had an image of Lorna and Chris's bedroom. All very modern with its Thai theme and silk sheets. How could they?

'So who was she,' said Lorna, 'the lady in the picture?'

'I don't know. I'm going to talk to George about it again when he gets back from school.'

'Have you shown the picture to the police?'

'No,' said Rachael, 'I suppose I should, but I just don't want him to be involved or questioned.'

'He's five, for goodness sake. Old enough to know what he's seen or heard. You should tell them.'

'OK, just leave it,' Rachael said.

Lorna's phone rang. She pulled it out of her pocket.

'Hello….yes, speaking….yes, yes, I see…….yes I can….yes I know where it is….I'll be there as soon as I can.'

She turned to Rachael, ashen faced.

'It's the Police, they want to talk to me.'

'I told you they would,' said Rachael.

'I'd better go,' said Lorna, standing up, 'I'm so sorry, Rachael. Bye'

'Yeah, bye,' said Rachael, turning her head away, as her sister walked out of sight.

Chapter Nine

The child was missing.

His grandmother turned up at the school to collect him, two weeks after Michael's murder, and he couldn't be found.

As she came through the gates, Miss Bonas had waved at her from the classroom door, where all the children were gathered, waiting for their parents to pick them up, but as she looked around for George, there was no sign of him.

'He was here a moment ago,' said Miss Bonas, flustered, 'he must have popped back into the school for something. Maybe he needed the toilet.'

George's grandmother had a sinking feeling. This wasn't right.

'Shall I go in and see if I can find him?' she asked.

'Oh, yes, if you could,' said Miss Bonas, 'the toilets are down the hall on the right. Or he may have left something in the classroom. It's got a penguin on the door. I'll be with you in a minute as soon as all the children have been collected.'

George's grandmother went into the school as fast as she could with her arthritic knee, and stared down the quiet empty corridor.

'George, George are you there?' she called as she checked the toilets and the class room. Both empty.

Her heart lurched as she looked at the peg on the wall with a brightly coloured 'George' above it. No coat or lunch box on it, just his blue stripy scarf that she'd knitted for him.

Where was he? Her mind went straight away to the worst scenario. Had he been taken by the woman who murdered Michael? Oh God, please let him be alright, she prayed.

Miss Bonas came hurrying in from the playground.

'Have you found him?' she asked, looking worried.

'No, he's not anywhere,' said George's grandmother, 'I think we should call the police.'

'Don't worry, I'm sure he'll turn up in a minute,' said Miss Bonas, concerned.

'I need to phone my daughter, she'll be expecting us home by three-thirty,' said George's grandmother, getting more and more panicked.

'Come into the office and use the school phone,' Miss Bonas said, showing her into a small room at the end of the corridor, 'I'm just going to have a quick check in all the classrooms and in the back playground, he does like the slide, I'm sure he'll be around somewhere.'

She rushed off, calling for a young assistant teacher to join in the search.

George's grandmother phoned Rachael, who picked up at once.

'Hi Mum, what's up?' she said, eating a piece of cake.

'Listen, don't panic, darling but we can't find George, Miss Bonas is going round the whole school to look for him.'

Rachael dropped the cake on the floor and grabbed the phone with both hands.

'What do you mean, you can't find him?'

'He's just disappeared. Oh, Rachael, I'm frightened something awful may have happened.'

'OK, Mum, I'm going to call the police. I've got a special number to get straight through to the murder team. I hope to God it hasn't got anything to do with Michael's death but the team need to know straight away just in case.'

'Alright Rachael, I'll phone you at once if he turns up,' she put the phone down and went to the door of the office and looked out.

'No luck yet, I'm afraid,' said Miss Bonas as she came running back down the corridor, 'but we're still looking.'

Within ten minutes a police car had turned up with the sirens wailing. George's grandmother had come over funny and was sitting on a chair in the office wondering if she was having a heart attack.

At the same time another police car had picked up Rachael from her parents' home and was scouring the streets round the school.

'Maybe George saw the murderer and she's worried that he might identify her so she's kidnapped him, so he can't,' Rachael said hysterically to the detective who was driving.

'Come on now, keep calm. I'm sure the boy will be fine. You need to just keep looking in all directions and think if there's anywhere he might have gone, or any friend that he might have gone home with. You know what kids are like, they sometimes forget to tell you.'

'He's only five,' said Rachael desperately.

'Does he know his way home from school?' the detective asked.

'To our house, yes, but not to my parents', where we're staying at the moment.'

'OK, let's go to your house and work our way back to the school.'

Rachael felt sick as they arrived at her house. She had the new key in her purse and felt an urge to go in and see if George was in there. Stupid, how could he be, he wouldn't be able to get in.

She looked up and down the street but couldn't see any sign of him.

'OK,' said the detective, 'direct me on the route you and George would take to school. How long does it take you to get there by car?'

'Only about ten minutes, but we did walk it once when the car was in the garage. Just go to the end of the road and turn right at the lights,' she said.

By now she had convinced herself that George was locked in a cellar somewhere and had been left to die. She was beside herself with panic, and the feeling of cold dread that invades you when you've lost a child.

As they turned the corner she suddenly saw him, a tiny figure walking slowly carrying his lunch box.

'Oh my God, there he is!' she shouted. 'Pull over, quickly pull over.'

The police car pulled in to the kerb and Rachael shot out of the passenger door and flung her arms round him. Hugging him for dear life.

'Georgie, I've been so worried about you. Where have you been?'

'Why are you crying, Mummy?' asked George, stroking her face.

'I thought I'd lost you,' she said, 'why didn't you wait for Nana?'

'I wasn't lost,' said George, 'I knew the way.'

'Where are you going?'

'I'm going home to get my box of Lego,' he said, 'I want to make some with Grandad.'

Chapter Ten

The woman sat by the fire with Kate. They'd cut up all the photos of Kate's injuries. The black eye, bruises to her face and breasts, the finger marks on the inside of her arms and thighs. Also one showing the scars along each of her wrists and another of her in the wheelchair.

Both of them were holding a cereal bowl containing some of the cut-up photos and they took it in turns to throw a small handful into the fire.

'They've been part of our lives for too long,' said the woman, 'it's time we let them go.'

'If only we'd found him sooner,' said Kate, throwing in another handful. She was careful not to look at them; she didn't want to be reminded of the horror of it all.

'I know, I think we could have set up an arrangement that would have kept us comfortable for quite a long time,' said the woman.

She'd noticed that Kate had been much calmer and more relaxed since the murder, finally able to stop worrying that the man might suddenly turn up and attack her again.

Kate was only seventeen when she was raped. Her father had vanished before she was born, so the woman had been left bringing her up on her own. Before it happened, they had done quite well, the two of them. Part-time jobs, here and there, a bit of shop-lifting, a few dodgy deals at car boot sales. Kate was a very pretty girl and people were always keen to help out. For five years, the woman also had a good blackmail scam running, concerning a 55 year old wealthy lady, who she had been cleaning for and found in bed with a wispy haired neighbour. The wife was terrified that her husband would find out and was well able to pay. The woman didn't feel too bad about it as she liked the old husband, who was kind and funny, and felt it only fair that her employer should pay for cheating on him. Sadly the wife then had a series of strokes and died, which left the woman having to jump off the gravy train.

Kate had always said she would recognise the man if she ever saw him again. She said she'd never forget his face or his voice. He'd approached her as she was leaving the gym, when she was seventeen, and asked her if she would like to feature in a video he was making about health and safety. She was flattered and he invited her to audition for the part of the main girl to be featured in the film.

She'd agreed to be collected by him outside the Health Club at 4pm the following day. He told her to dress nicely, with good make-up and hair. He was well-spoken, wore a suit and was quite good looking for an older man. She reckoned he must be about thirty. She was incredibly excited but didn't tell her mother because she knew she'd only want to come with her and that would be really embarrassing. Anyway, she felt she could take care of herself.

He picked her up the next day in his car as planned and as they were driving along, he talked all about the film and what her part in it would be. She was hanging on every word and not taking in where they were going. The car suddenly turned into an underground car park with only two other cars in it.

'Out we get,' he said, and led her to a small lift that took them up to the second floor.

'Here we are,' he said opening a door with his key and ushering her into what looked like a posh office or waiting room.

There was no-one else there and Kate began to feel a little uneasy.

'The others will be along later,' he said, 'but before they arrive, we need to take a few pictures of you to see how you look on camera.'

'First of all a glass of champagne,' he went on, going to a small fridge and bringing out a bottle.

Kate had never had real champagne before and felt very sophisticated as she took a sip but didn't really like the taste and put her glass down on a low table set against the wall.

He got her to pose for a few photos in various exercise positions, saying, 'very good, yes, that's great, perfect,' each time. He had a big camera on a tripod, set up in the middle of the room.

She was wearing a short skirt and a tight top with her push-up bra underneath.

'Right, now just slip your top and skirt off and we can get a few shots to show them what a lovely body you have.'

'Oh, no,' said Kate, panicking, ' I didn't realise that….'

'Come on now, don't be shy, you have to suffer for your art if you want to get on in show business, you know,' he said laughing.

She nervously took her top off, feeling very vulnerable and embarrassed.

'Perfect,' he said taking more photographs, just move your shoulders together and give me a kiss for the camera.'

'When are the others coming,' she asked, 'when do we start the audition?'

'This is the audition, sweetheart, I decide whether you get the job. Now take your skirt off and don't be a silly girl.'

'No,' she said, reaching for her top, 'I won't. I want to go home.'

That was when it happened. He came over and hit her hard across the face.

'Oh no you don't. I'm not wasting my time for nothing. You do as I say and keep your mouth shut about it afterwards, or

I'll show the photos I've just taken to all your friends and family to show them what a little tart you are.'

He pushed her back onto the leather sofa, pulled up her skirt and then took her pants off, in one deft move. She struggled and tried to fight him off but he was too strong for her. He hit her in the face and then kept slapping her, while he forced himself into her, thrusting hard and causing her terrible pain.

She tried to scream but he put his hand over her mouth.

'If you scream I'll hit you again,' he said, 'do you want that?'

She shook her head, sobbing and gasping for breath.

'Good girl,' he said, 'you just let me do what I want and it'll soon be over.'

When he'd finally finished he got up and poured himself another glass of champagne.

Kate lay there in a crumpled heap, sobbing.

'It's all part of life's learning curve, sweetheart,' he said, 'didn't your mother ever tell you not to go off with strange men?'

His phone rang and he answered it, turning away from her.

'What *now*?' he said, angrily into the phone, 'well what time will you be here? OK, I'll see you then.'

'Damn,' he said, looking at his watch. He turned to Kate, 'come on get dressed, you have to leave. Wipe your face with this, you look terrible.' He flung her a small grey towel, 'I'll drop you off near the Gym.'

Kate stumbled to her feet, pulled down her skirt and managed to get her pants and top on. She grabbed her bag, picked her bra up off the floor, and then he pulled her out of the flat and into the lift.

'Put these on,' he ordered, handing her a pair of dark glasses.

He dropped her off round the back of the gym, opening the car door for her as she stumbled out.

'Bye, 'blue eyes', take care,' he said, pulling the dark glasses off her face and kissing her wetly on the mouth. Then he climbed back into his car and drove off.

Kate sank back against the fence. Thankful to be alive but shaking from head to foot.

'Are you all right, love?' a man asked, as he passed by, a few minutes later.

'Yes, I'm fine,' she answered, shrinking back from him and covering her face with her hand.

'OK, keep your hair on, just asking,' he said, as he went on past her.

She managed to get herself home, take off her clothes and put them for a wash in the machine, then have a bath before her mother came back...she felt damaged and dirty and couldn't stop crying.

She told her mother everything that had happened.

The woman was beside herself with rage.

'The bastard,' she kept saying.

'Should I go to the police?' Kate asked her tearfully.

'No. I'll handle this,' her mother said.

She knew that it would be horrendous for Kate to be physically examined and questioned by the police after everything that she had been through. Anyway, she'd already had a bath and put her clothes through the machine, which would have washed away any remaining evidence, and even if they found the man and it came to court, Kate wouldn't have a leg to stand on, since she'd gone back to the man's place voluntarily.

'What are you going to do?' asked Kate.

'One way or another I will find him and make his life a living hell,' she said, grimly.

§

It had taken this long, but as they sat by the fire, ten years later, throwing in the cut-up photos, the woman thought to herself, well, I wasn't able to make him suffer long term, but at least he had a horrible violent death and he won't be able to damage any more young girls.

She'd done what she could.

Chapter Eleven

'I want to go alone.'

Rachael's mother looked at her, anxiously.

'Are you sure,' she said, 'I'm happy to come with you.'

'No thanks, Mum, I'll be fine. It's something I need to do.'

The thought of entering her house after everything that had happened there, made her feel sick, but she was determined to face it.

She'd finally got rid of the cast on her wrist and was able to drive again. It was wonderful to be free to go wherever she wanted, without having to depend on her parents, or take buses or taxis. She felt back in control. In fact she was beginning to feel a growing sense of calm, despite what had happened to Michael. She was her own person again. Not having to report everything she did, back to him. Not having to live with the fear of him and the loneliness of keeping a dark secret that she couldn't tell anyone.

But as she drove up to No 6 and parked outside, she got a churning feeling in her stomach. Silly; he couldn't hurt her now. She got out and went up the steps to the front door. She managed to make the new key work OK and as soon as she stepped inside she disarmed the new alarm system. She'd been worried that it would be too complicated. That bells would start ringing and she wouldn't know how to stop them, but luckily it worked fine.

She shut the door and stood still for a moment. The house smelled different. The hall carpet looked cleaner than ever before. She took off her jacket and hung it on a hook and put her keys in the bowl on the hall table. Old familiar patterns, and yet everything had changed so much. There was a pile of post on the mat, which she gathered up into a pile to take away and sort out later.

She took a deep breath and entered the living room.

She half expected to see Michael, lying in a sea of blood. But no, everything was in order. The crime scene cleaners had done a brilliant job. The table had been cleared and the wooden floor was back to normal apart from the very faintest stain of faded brown that they hadn't been able to remove. There was a rug missing, which they'd told her needed to be disposed of, on health grounds.

It was basically two good sized rooms that had been opened out into one large one. She looked at the living area with its log fire and elegant, duck egg blue sofa and chairs. Although she loved the house, she didn't think she could ever come back and live here again, after what had happened.

She opened the big window overlooking the garden, and also the top half of the one facing the street. She wanted the fresh air to erase everything that had gone on inside. It was late

September and there was quite a chill, but it felt good allowing the wind to blow through.

She went to her pine desk in the corner and fished out the house file. She couldn't face getting down close to the floor where Michael had been lying, to measure the dining area, but she still had the estate agent's 'print out' of the house from when they bought it, with all the room sizes. She found it quickly and put it in her bag. She would drop by the carpet shop on her way home and order a carpet to be fitted to the whole room. Cream, she thought. It would give the room a whole new fresh look.

Even though there would be a significant price drop because of the murder, she thought she might let the house and find somewhere small to rent locally, for her and George, until all the details of the will and the inquest were resolved.

She went upstairs to George's room. Bless him, he was such a little character. Her heart ached as she put some of his favourite toys into a big blue plastic bag. His box of Lego, some of his favourite books, a few dinosaurs, and his cuddly donkey 'Eeyore' who was still tucked under the duvet on his bed with one ear flopping out.

She left the bag on the landing ready to take back to her parents' house and was about to go into her bedroom when she suddenly heard a noise downstairs. Her heart started pounding. She kept very still, waiting to hear any other sounds. Had Michael's murderer seen her arrive, climbed in through the open windows downstairs and come in to kill her?

Then she heard a miaow and realised it was next door's cat who had decided to come in and see what was going on.

'Oh, for God's sake Midas you nearly gave me a heart attack,' she said to him as he ran up the stairs and wound himself round her legs for a stroke.

She'd always wanted to have a cat but Michael had vetoed it, 'too messy,' he'd said.

OK, this was the big one. She went into the bedroom, armed with a roll of green plastic garden bags. She opened his side of the wardrobe and looked at all his clothes hanging on the rail as if waiting for him to come and choose them.

She took them off the hangers one by one and stuffed them quickly into two of the bags. It was almost as if she was in a trance. She went to his drawers and put his t-shirts, underwear, and socks into another bag and finally, she was going to throw all his shoes and boots into the big backpack, which she'd pulled from the top of the wardrobe, when she noticed that a photo had floated to the floor. It was of a teenage girl in just her pants and bra looking really embarrassed.

The hairs on the back of her neck stood up.

She got a chair, climbed up and felt along the top of the wardrobe and found two more photos of different girls of a similar age, both partially undressed. One had her back to the camera and was wearing only her jeans with her hands over her breasts and her head half turned, awkwardly, back to the photographer, and the other was in her school uniform with the

74

buttons of her shirt undone and nothing underneath except her tie. None of the girls looked as if they were happy to have their photos taken.

'Oh God, Michael, what did you do?' she whispered, her hand up to her mouth.

She would have to take them straight to the police. Somewhere, somehow they must be connected to the murder. Had he raped them? Had he killed them?

She lugged the heavy bags of his clothes out onto the landing and kicked them down the stairs, followed by his backpack.

'Gone,' she said, as she watched them roll all the way down to the bottom. She'd drop them off at the dump on the way home after she'd taken the photos into the police station.

She went into the bathroom and scooped his toiletries into his sponge bag, then took it and George's toys downstairs and put them all by the front door. She took the three photos of the girls into the kitchen and started to make herself a cup of tea. She was feeling really shaky. She looked in the fridge. Empty. The crime scene cleaners must have cleared it for her. She checked the freezer. Full. Oh, hell, she'd better take some of that frozen food back to her parents.

It suddenly all became too much for her. So many things to sort out, so many things to do. And now these photos of young girls. It was just horrible. She sat the kitchen table, put her head on her arms and started to cry. She wished she'd brought her mum with her. After a bit she pulled herself together and found some long-life milk in the cupboard and made a cup of tea. She felt weak and wobbly as if she might collapse, then she found a packet of shortbread biscuits and ate through them all.

She caught sight of a photo on the fridge door of her and Lorna with Mum and Dad from a few Christmases ago. She peeled it off, tore it into bits, and threw the pieces into the bin. She still couldn't believe that Michael and her sister had been having an affair and that she had never even suspected it. How could she have been so stupid. The police had told her that Lorna was now eliminated from their enquiries, but they hadn't spoken to each other since they'd met by the pond. Lorna had finally told their parents about her affair with Michael because she didn't want them to hear about it from the police. They had been horrified of course, but she knew they'd forgive Lorna after a bit. They always did.

There was also a photo of her and Michael on holiday in Tunisia, holding a glass of wine each, over dinner. That one had to go. She remembered that he had insisted on sex that night even though she had been feeling ill. He wouldn't hit her while they were away because he liked her to be in her bikini by the pool, so no marks or bruises until they got home. Eventually she got a plastic bag from under the sink and put all the fridge photos in it to throw away, only keeping the ones of her and George.

She took her tea into the living room and sat on the sofa, looking again at the photos of the three girls.

Suddenly the phone rang. She stared at it, not wanting to talk to anybody. After six rings it cut to the answer phone message.

Michael's voice suddenly seemed to fill the room.

'I'm sorry, there's no-one here to take your call. Please leave a message. I'll get back to you later.'

It felt like a threat.

He would get back to her later.

Chapter Twelve

George had made a friend at school.

A boy called Angus had arrived a week after term started and was in the other class. He had red hair and some of the boys had started to tease him about it. The child saw him crying in the playground one day at break time and went up to him.

'What's the matter?' he asked.

'Those boys were being horrid to me,' the boy said, sniffing and wiping his nose on the back of his hand.

'Do you want a sweet?' said George fishing a rather grubby one out of his pocket.

'Yes, please,' said the boy, giving him a shy smile and taking it.

'What's your name?' George asked.

'Angus, what's yours?'

'George.'

Angus popped the sweet in his mouth.

'Do you want to be my friend?' said George.

'Yes please,' said Angus.

'Shall we play on the 'trim trail', there's no-one on it?'

'Alright,' said Angus cheering up a bit.

'Come on then,' said George running across the playground and jumping on.

Angus followed and they jumped from log to log, laughing as they went.

After that they played together every break-time.

§

Three days later they were sitting on some big coloured boxes that they'd climbed. They sat next to each other with their legs hanging over the edge.

'My daddy's gone away and isn't ever coming back,' said George.

'Is he dead?' asked Angus.

'I don't think so.'

'Oh,' said Angus, 'where's he gone?'

'I don't know, America, probably.'

'Wow,' said Angus, impressed.

'Yes, he's going to Disney World,' added George.

'My daddy climbed a big mountain,' said Angus, 'and he's very clever.'

'Well my daddy got stabbed in the stomach by a lady with a knife and I saw it!'

Angus thought about this for a minute.

'Did you?' he said admiringly.

'Yes, that's why he had to go away.' said George.

Angus thought a bit more.

'What did your mummy say?'

'She wasn't there, she was at the hospital.'

'Why?' asked Angus.

'Daddy pushed her and she hurt her arm.'

'Well, my mummy fell down the stairs and banged her face and there was blood on her nightie,' said Angus.

George remembered his mummy's nose bleeding.

'Does your daddy hit your mummy?' he asked.

'No, he lives in Scotland,' said Angus, picking a scab on his knee.

'Where's Scotland?'

'A million zillion miles away,' said Angus.

George didn't say anything.

The bell went, so they climbed down and ran back towards the classrooms.

'Do you want to come back to my house after school for tea?' shouted Angus as they ran.

'Yes please,' said George, taking big jumping strides back to his class.

§

As the children came out of school, George went rushing up to Rachael.

'Mummy, I've got a friend and he wants me to go back to his house for tea,' he said excitedly.

Rachael saw a woman who she'd noticed in the playground before and thought looked nice, approaching them with a small red haired boy who was pulling her by the hand and pointing at Rachael and George.

'Hi, I'm Clare,' the mother said to Rachael, with a warm smile, 'the boys seem to have made friends and Angus really wants George to come back for a play. Any chance? I only live round the corner.'

'Well, that'd be great, but...' said Rachael, hesitating a bit, wondering if it was too soon and if he might be a bit too young to cope with it on his own.

'I tell you what, why don't you come as well and have a cup of tea?' said Clare, as if reading her thoughts, 'if you've got time, that is.'

'Today?' asked Rachael.

'Why not?' said Clare.

'Please,' begged both the boys in unison. Clare and Rachael laughed.

'You can have a go on my scooter,' Angus said to George.

Rachael saw his face light up. It would be good for him to have a friend, she thought, to help him to take his mind off everything.

'Well, if you're sure,' she said, smiling at Clare, 'that would be lovely.'

'Follow me,' said Clare, 'where are you parked?'

'Down Northcote Avenue,' said Rachael.

'Perfect,' said Clare, 'that's our road! Number 41, half way down.'

'I've just got to give my mum a quick ring to let her know we'll be late back,' said Rachael getting out her phone.

'No problem,' said Clare, walking on a bit with the boys.

The whole school had heard about George's father being murdered and she felt so sorry for Rachael. What must the poor woman be going through.

Angus took her hand and looked up at her.

'Thank you Mummy,' he said, hopping up and down excitedly on one foot, 'I've got lots of things to tell you.'

Chapter Thirteen

As the weeks passed, the woman began to feel less anxious. There had been no further news in the papers about the murder. No-one had come knocking at their door. No surprise calls from the police.

She'd got away with it, she thought to herself, sitting in her Renault in the car park, her phone by her side, ready to take some photos of the couple a short distance away who were having a torrid session of give and take in their Volvo.

Since her visit to Michael had gone so disastrously wrong, she had been looking out for another blackmail victim to turn up and this could be the perfect solution. She really needed to find a way to get more money.

Recently, since Michael's death, Kate had begun to be more like her old self.

After her ordeal at the hands of that horrible man, Kate had changed so much. She'd become frightened of leaving the house. Didn't want to finish college, had stopped wearing make-up and doing fancy hairstyles. Just sat in her room for months, crying and staying in her pyjamas for most of the day watching TV.

She said she didn't ever want to have a boyfriend and had freaked out on the one occasion when the woman had brought a man friend back to the house, after a night out.

Then came the awful day about two years after the rape when Kate had cut her wrists in the bath. Fortunately she had found her in time but she'd had to call an ambulance and get her to hospital. They'd stitched her up and asked a lot of questions. Had she had a row with her boyfriend? Was it the pressure of exams? Did she suffer from depression?

In the end they sent her home the next day and told her to contact their G.P. as soon as possible. He asked all the same questions and ended up giving her a prescription for Prozac.

Kate hated taking the pills. They made her go into a zombie state and after a few weeks, the woman helped her to flush them down the toilet and they decided that they would find a way through without them.

Slowly, Kate began to get better and sometimes it seemed as if she had got over it. But there was no way that the woman could. Each time she looked at her daughter's thin scarred wrists her heart twisted and she was filled with hate for the bastard who had done this to her daughter.

She'd tried for months to find out who he was, but never with any success, until the moment when Kate saw him on television and had called her to come and see. The woman was shocked that he looked quite normal. In her mind she had developed an image of him looking like an evil monster.

Well. She'd found him and she'd done for him. She had no regrets. Men like that needed to be removed from the face of the earth.

§

When he'd opened the door to her on the night of the murder he'd been charm itself, to start with.

'Can I help you?' he asked politely.

'I wonder if I could have a few words with you in private?'

'Yes, of course,' he said, ushering her into the hall and on into the living room, pulling the door to behind him. 'Now, tell me what it is you want to talk about,' he went on, flashing a practised smile at her, 'if it's to do with the tree outside, I've already been in touch with the council.'

'No, it's not about the tree, it's about my daughter,' she said firmly.

She saw a flash of alarm cross his face, which quickly morphed into a smile.

'Yes?' he said smoothly, 'do go on.'

'Ten years ago, when she was only fifteen, you told her you wanted to audition her for a role in a film. You took her back to your flat and you…'

His face paled and then flooded with colour.

86

'Stop right there,' he said angrily, 'I've no idea what you're talking about. Now get out of my house, before I call the police.'

'Oh yes, call the police, good idea,' the woman said, standing her ground, years of pent up rage bursting up to the surface, 'I'll tell them how you violently attacked and raped her. I'll tell them she's never really recovered. That she's tried to commit suicide not once but twice.'

Kate had actually been seventeen not fifteen, and only tried to kill herself once, but how could he have known that. Let him squirm.

'You've got the wrong person. It couldn't possibly have been me.'

'She's seen you on television and is prepared to formally identify you,' said the woman.

'She's lying,' he shouted, his temper rising and his face sweating.

'Her name is Kate, do you remember? Or have there been so many girls you've lost track? Look I'll show you some photos to jog your memory.'

She pulled one out of her bag, holding it high above her head.

'This is her covered in bruises on her face, arms and thighs.'

She took out another, a close-up of Kate's bruised breasts.
'Just look. She was fifteen for God's sake.'

'Give those to me,' he snarled, lunging at her.

She dodged him and pulled out another one showing Kate's wrists with the stitches looking red and angry against her pale skin.

'I didn't do that,' he shouted.

He was getting scared now, she saw.

'No, *she* did; because of what you did to her. She tried to kill herself.'

He reached for the photo but she side-stepped him.

She held up the last photo, of Kate in her wheelchair holding her hands out, palms upward and showing the silver white scars.

'She's in a wheelchair now,' the woman went on, 'she's an amputee. She lost her leg after she'd jumped out of a window. She was that desperate.'

She was quite enjoying twisting the facts.

'I've never seen her before in my life, you stupid woman. What do you want from me?' he asked, looking at her angrily.

'I'm going to show these to the police and tell them everything you've done, unless you pay a £1000 a month to help me look after her. It's the least you can do, you bastard.'

His face changed and he advanced slowly towards her.

'Oh, I get it. No, you don't, you bitch. You don't pin that on me. So that's it, you think you can blackmail me, do you? That's a crime as well, you know. Well, I'm not going to pay a penny to you or your wretched daughter. She's a plain little thing, isn't she, not worth the effort, I'd say.'

He came towards her, reaching again for the photos.

The woman quickly stuffed them in her bag and backed away from him.

'Give them to me, you stupid cow,' he said, raising his arm and suddenly striking her across the face with the back of his hand.

The room swam for a moment.

He got hold of her hair, which was tied back in a low bun, and forced her across the room and back against the table, then started banging her head against it. Hard. His other hand was round her throat. She started to panic.

'If you ever - try - anything - like this - again,' he shouted, 'I swear to God I'll kill you.'

§

Well, it hadn't quite worked out like that, thought the woman, as she remembered that night.

She sat in her car with the lights off, watching the couple making out in the Volvo. The girl looking so young and the man had his silver hair all askew. This could be the answer. They would have to pay for the sins they were committing. Good.

She had a plan.

Chapter Fourteen

The morning after George and Rachael had gone back for tea, Clare came up to Rachael at the school gates, after they'd dropped the children off.

'Oh hi,' she said, 'have you got a moment, I really need to talk to you.'

'Yes, of course,' said Rachael, 'what about?'

'Look, come back and have a coffee and I'll explain. It's about some things that George said to Angus.'

Rachael's heart sank. Oh God what had he been saying.

They didn't talk any more until they were in Clare's house.

As they sat together at the kitchen table, Clare handed her a cup of coffee.

'I'm so sorry,' she said, 'I had no idea that George had actually witnessed the murder.'

Rachael's blood ran cold.

'He didn't,' she said, 'he was asleep upstairs.'

'Oh,' said Clare, biting her lip, 'it's just that he told Angus he'd seen a woman pushing a knife into his daddy.'

Rachael covered her mouth with her hand.

'Perhaps he was just making it up,' |Clare went on quickly, 'but I felt I needed to tell you what he'd said.'

'Thanks,' said Rachael.

Surely George would have told her, if he'd seen Michael being stabbed. Perhaps he'd thought he'd get into trouble or something. But how else would he know about the knife? Who could have told him? They'd been so careful to keep the details from him.

'He's never told me he saw anything,' she said, 'but maybe he did and was just afraid to say. There's something else, too.'

She told Clare about the picture that George had drawn with 'Daddy and the lady'.

'I was thinking that maybe he'd seen Michael with another woman at some time but now I'm wondering …'

'Why wouldn't he tell you, if he'd seen something?' asked Clare.

'Well you know what they're like,' Rachael said, absently, thinking that she'd have to go and tell the police about this. She'd protected George as long as she could but now she realised that the detectives needed to talk to him. He had to explain more about the picture, and if he had seen the murder then perhaps he could give them a clue as to what the woman looked like. Poor George, what a terrible secret to have kept all these weeks.

'He also told Angus that your broken wrist was caused by your husband pushing you, and that he hit you,' Clare went on, apologetically, 'I don't know if that's true, but if it is, I just wanted to let you know that I understand,' she went on, 'I left my first husband because he was violent towards me.'

Rachael looked at Clare. She looked so well and confident. Could she really have been through a similar situation to herself? Did she really know what it was like? As she looked at Clare's concerned, intense face she thought, yes, she's been there. She knows.

Slowly she began to unburden herself to Clare. She told her all about the abuse she had suffered from Michael. It was such a relief to be able to tell someone in detail about everything she had been through. And so much easier to talk to a person who knew nothing about her life. Clare listened and nodded in sympathy.

'You could be telling me my own story from ten years ago,' she said eventually, 'well, whatever happened to cause your husband's death, and however awful it must have been for you to find him like that, at least you don't have to be frightened of him any more.'

She leant across the table and took Rachael's hand.

'You've got me on your side now,' she said, 'I'll do everything I can to help you get back on your feet. You can call me whenever you like and you must let me know if you want help with George at any time, he can always come here and play with Angus.'

'Thanks,' said Rachael, feeling as if she was going to cry, 'I'm just so scared about everything,' she went on, shakily.

'I know,' said Clare, 'but you'll find a way to move on. It's not easy but you will.'

Rachael felt a rush of gratitude. To have met a woman in the midst of all this mayhem, who she felt could trust and might even become a close friend, was like a miracle.

'Thank you so much, I can't begin to tell you what it means.'

'That's OK,' said Clare, 'I know what it's like; it was a terrible time in my life. Thankfully, my second husband, Finn, George's father, wasn't violent in any way - just disinterested, really!'

'Where is he now?' Rachael asked her.

'He's up in Edinburgh. Since the divorce we haven't had much contact. Apart from the times when he comes to see George, which is not very often. We managed to keep it out of the courts and we agreed that he would have George for a week at Easter and two weeks during the summer holidays, plus the occasional weekend. So far, none of that's happened. He just drops by occasionally to say hello if he has to come to

London,' she laughed wryly, 'he a very busy man with not much free time. That was part of our problem!'
'What does he do?'

'He runs mountaineering courses. He's very keen on climbing. He made it to the top of Everest once!'

'How does Angus feel about it all?' asked Rachael.

'Well, he seems OK. He gets upset if his father can't come to see him when he's promised that he would, but other than that, he seems to have accepted the situation for what it is.'

'That's something, I suppose.'

'I'm just glad if they can keep their relationship going, even if it's only a slight connection. He's not an easy man but at least we're on speaking terms. He has a new partner now and she has a son, I gather. I wonder how much time Finn gets to spend with him!'

Rachael suddenly felt really sad for her new friend. To go through an abusive marriage and then on to another where she wasn't treasured or appreciated. And to know that he'd now found love with someone else. She felt a cold shiver running through her. Life was difficult.

'I'll be here for you too, in any way I can,' she said.

'Thanks,' said Clare, giving her a hug.

Chapter Fifteen

As Rachael was putting George to bed that night, she decided she must tackle it straight on.

'So,' she said, tucking Eeyore in with him under the duvet, 'did you and Angus have a good play in his room yesterday?'

'Yes,' said George, 'we played with his train set, he's got lots and lots.'

'Lucky him,' said Rachael, 'and did you talk about all sorts of things?'

'Course we did,' said George, laughing at her.

'Did you tell him about what happened to Daddy?'

She could feel her heart hammering in her chest.

George looked at her for a moment.

'Daddy's not coming back, is he?' he said seriously.

'No darling he's not.'

George was silent for a moment.

'Is Daddy dead?' he said, 'that's what the boys at school are saying.'

Oh my God, how had that got through to a class of five year-olds? Well it's better he knows the truth, thought Rachael, he's going to find out someday anyway.

'Yes, darling, I'm afraid Daddy is dead. Sometimes awful things happen. I'm so sorry.'

'I don't mind, Mummy,' George said, 'can you read me a story now?'

'In a minute, sweetheart, I just wanted to ask you if you knew what actually happened to Daddy?'

'Well,' said George with a look of concentration on his face, 'I saw a lady push a knife in his tummy, but I don't know how he got dead.'

Rachael tried to keep her voice calm.

'How did you see that?' she asked.

'I was peeping,' said George, looking down and hanging his head.

'Peeping?'

'Yes, the door was open a little bit and I could see.'

'Why didn't you tell me?' asked Rachael.

'You were at the hospital.'

'Why didn't you tell me in the morning?'

'Well, Daddy would be cross with me, because I was out of bed.'

'But you could have told me,' she said, pushing his hair back from his face.

'You were sad, Mummy and you had a hurty arm.'

She kissed him on the forehead.

'What did the lady look like?' she said. She knew she might be pushing her luck but he was at least talking about it.

'She looked a bit like Miss Harold, but it wasn't her.'

'Miss Harold?' said Rachael, surprised.

Miss Harold was the headmistress at George's school. She was about fifty-five years old, rather overweight, with greying black hair that she wore back in a bun. Quite severe looking.

'What was she wearing?' she asked.

'I don't know.'

'Did she have trousers on or a skirt?'

George laughed.

'A skirt of course.'
'What colour?'

'I can't remember. Sort of bluey. Can I have my story now?' he asked, his eyes beginning to close.

'Of course you can, darling,' Rachael said, picking up the book they'd chosen from the library, about a bull who wanted to sniff flowers instead of fighting.

'Right,' she began, 'Once upon a time…'

Chapter Sixteen

The police were Immediately interested when Rachael phoned them the next day. She told them that George had told a friend that he had seen his father being stabbed.

They came round to her parents house the same day to talk to George as soon as he got back from school. They brought with them a friendly looking woman, called Angie, who was a Family Liaison Officer. George took to her immediately. She had a kind face and had brought him a brand new drawing pad, felt-tipped pens and some play-dough.

The detectives had already talked to him previously about the drawing of his father and 'the lady' but hadn't got much out of him. He'd been a bit shy and reserved with them.

This time it was different. He seemed happier to talk about things, especially to Angie. The whole conversation was being discreetly recorded by the detectives.

'So what happened to your Daddy?' she asked, after they'd played a few games together.

'He's dead,' said George.

'Oh,' she said nodding, 'did you see him die?'

'No,' said George.

'So what did you see?' she asked moulding some play-dough in her fingers and making a tree.

'He was having a fight with a lady and then she pushed a knife into his tummy.'

'Oh, what sort of knife, was it?' Angie asked.

'Just one off the table,' said George, trying to make a dog with the yellow dough. The legs kept falling off.

Rachael was standing at the back of the room with the detectives. Her heart was racing. This was the last thing she had wanted, for George to become a key witness. But she kept silent, Angie seemed to be handling it well, so far.

'Who was the lady, then?' Angie asked, casually, helping him fix the legs on.

'I don't know,' said George.

'What did she look like,' she asked.

'Like Miss Harold,' he said, making a huge ear and sticking it on.

'Who's she?' Angie asked, 'your girlfriend?'

'No,' said George screaming with laughter, 'she's the headmistress at my school.'

'So what's she like?'

'She's fat and old and cross,' said George.

Rachael winced. Poor Miss Harold.

'Was she wearing a huge red dress?' asked Angie, smiling.

'No, she was wearing a blue skirt and top, silly.'

'So how did you see what what was happening,' said Angie.

'I was in the hall. The door was open a bit and I could see through. I should have been in bed but I came down in case it was Mummy coming home.'

'Where had Mummy been, then?' asked Angie, adding a leaf to her tree.

'At the hospital. Daddy hit her and pushed her over and she hurt her hand.'

Rachael started to move towards them, but one of the detectives restrained her gently but firmly.

'Daddy didn't ever hit you though, did he?' Angie asked, starting to make a flower.

'Sometimes he did, but not like he hit Mummy. Oh, here's his tail,' he went on, pressing a large bit of red dough onto the dog's backside.

Rachael put her hand up to her mouth. Well, the truth was out now.

'Did you see anything else?' Angie asked.

'No, I ran back upstairs to bed in case Daddy saw me.'

'Right,' said Angie, 'so what shall we do now?'

'Squash the dog,' said George laughing and bringing his hand down hard onto the dog and flattening it.

Chapter Seventeen

The woman would take her time, stalking her new prey.

If there was to be a good blackmail scam, she had to know everything about the couple in the Volvo and have as much photographic evidence as she could.

She sat in the car with her lights off and the driver's window open, looking as if she was busy on her phone. She was. She took a photo of their car and of the number plate. There was little chance that they would notice her as they were deeply entwined. The young blonde had taken her top off and had only a thin camisole on. She had her head tipped back and her eyes closed. The silver -haired man was burying his head in her cleavage and leaning over with his right arm in her lap. The woman got a perfect short video of what they were up to and had a great view of the girl's face. After a minute or two the man lifted his head and looked up at the girl. Yes. Click. The woman got a clear shot of his face, as well. His hair all rumpled and his cheeks flushed.

She sat back and waited. After a while their car lights came on and they drove out of the car park.

The woman followed them at a discreet distance. She managed to get one car between her and them to throw them off the scent and kept following them at a steady distance until they indicated left. She took the same turning and soon found herself right behind them. She could see they were in deep conversation. The girl had her hand on the back of the man's neck and her left arm stretched over onto his lap. Careful girl, the woman thought. Sexually charged young women in passenger seats needed to be banned, as much as talking on mobiles.

They indicated right and as they turned, her access was blocked by an oncoming car. Shit. Had she lost them? She followed as soon as she could and sped up, seeing them going round the corner three cars ahead of her. She took the same turn and found herself in a smaller road, with their car pulling in to the left. She drove on past them and pulled in to the right a few cars further up.

She turned off her lights and in the driving mirror, she saw the girl hop out and run up to the front door. She got her key from her purse and entered, turning to give a small wave to the man, before shutting the door. Great. Now she knew where the girl lived. The man appeared to be making a phone call and the woman was able to take a photo of the house. Number 28.

She was really enjoying herself. She had always rather fancied being a private investigator. Maybe she'd take it up someday, it could be a good way to make money, she thought, without the fear of getting hauled in by the police for fingerprints. It had become something of a mantra for her since the murder. No fingerprints, no fingerprints, she chanted under her breath, beating her hand in time on the driving wheel. By mistake, she sounded the horn. She nearly jumped out of her skin. Damn. She looked back and could see the man turn his head and look around to see where the beep had come from. She ducked down. He started his car at once and drove past her. She knew she was pushing her luck but she couldn't resist pulling out and following him, noting the name of the road as she passed.

She followed him for about fifteen minutes until he drew up outside a small but smart detached house, with double gates standing open onto a white chip drive. As he drove in, the front door opened and an attractive woman, of about forty-five, came out followed by two children with bare feet; a girl of about ten, in her nightie and a boy of about eight in his pyjamas. Second marriage, the woman guessed as she pulled up on the other side of the road.

The family waited until he'd got out of the car and walked up to the front porch, the children jumping up and down with excitement, giving him a hug as he put his arms round them. He gave his wife a quick peck on the cheek. A peck, thought the woman, watching from her car. How dare he.

She managed to get a quick shot of them all on her phone and then drove away before anyone noticed her.

Gotcha, she thought. But no rush. Next she had to find out who he was and where he worked. What were the pressure points that she could apply? Did they only meet in car parks or were there opportunities elsewhere? In a hotel? In either of their houses? Was the girl married or in another relationship, where did she work, how much damage would the revelation of their affair do to either of them?

Oh, yes, she thought as she drove home to Kate, turning the radio on. She had plenty of work to do.

Chapter Eighteen

It was five a.m. and Rachael lay wide awake, in her small teenage bed, with George sleeping peacefully in the one next to her. Her mind was going round and round, trying to make sense of everything that was happening.

All hell was breaking loose with Lorna and Chris.

Chris had been called in for questioning and had learnt about Lorna's affair with Michael. He had gone ballistic. Quiet estate agent turned furious, vindictive, cuckolded husband. They'd had a massive row and he had turned her out of their flat, throwing all her clothes and possessions off the small balcony and onto the communal lawn. Thai silk bed cushions and candles mixing with dirty washing, shoes, DVDs, underwear, books, and clothes that he had drenched with toilet cleaner and could never be worn again. His last words, shouted to her from the balcony were 'if I'd have known about your filthy affair I would have killed him myself, it's just a shame someone got there first.'

Lorna had been hysterical and driven back to her parents' house and was now sleeping on their sofa.

Her parents were doing their best to cope but their lives had been turned upside down as well. First by the shock of the murder, then by Rachael and George coming to stay, and now Lorna as well. The house was a shambles, with piles of Lorna's stuff pushed against the wall in the sitting room and extra pillows and blankets, all stuffed behind the sofa.

Rachael decided enough was enough and made the decision to bite the bullet and move back into her old house with George. All other options seemed too complicated at this stage. How do you let or sell a house where there's been a widely publicised recent murder? The new cream carpet had been fitted in the sitting room but even so....

She wasn't sure enough of her finances to rent somewhere new and she desperately needed her own space. Apart from anything else she felt she could no longer live in the same house as Lorna.

Once she and George had moved back home, she would try and get a part-time job as an office temp. Just something to keep her going until she found out how she was going to end up, financially. All being well she would eventually be able to sell the house and use what money was left to plan the next stage in her life.

She'd been suffering with insomnia since Michael's death. She kept getting flashbacks of finding him lying in a pool of blood. She still felt guilty, but because of everything he'd done to her, she couldn't feel any grief. Perhaps it would be easier once they'd got the funeral over and done with. Maybe, when she sold the house, she would take George and spend a year travelling round Europe. After all, she would be free to do whatever she wanted. The thought of it filled her with a sudden excitement. What if she could persuade Clare and Angus to come with them? That would be fantastic.

Thelma and Louise - and George and Angus!

§

Later on, after dropping George off at school, she came back and found Lorna trying to tidy up some of her things in the sitting room. She could hear their Mum clattering about in the kitchen and she told Lorna that she was planning to move out as soon as possible.

'Oh God,' said Lorna, 'I feel awful, I've made everything worse, haven't I?'

'It's not just because of you,' Rachael said, 'it's too much for Mum and Dad having us both here and with George as well, and anyway I really need to be on my own for a bit now.'

'Are you sure,' said Lorna, 'I would hate to think it was my fault that you have to leave.'

'It's OK,' said Rachael, not wanting to go there, 'I'll move out at the weekend and you can have our old room back.'

'What am I going to do,' Lorna said, sinking onto the sofa. She started to cry, her shoulders shaking, 'how am I going to live?'

'You'll find a way,' said Rachael, unable to rustle up much sympathy.

Chapter Nineteen

When she got home from her adventures, tracking the courting couple, the woman could hear voices coming from the sitting room and then Kate's giggle, followed by a male laugh.

What the hell was this? Kate should be sitting quietly on the sofa with her leg up on the coffee table, watching 'The Voice' and working her way through the bag of popcorn that she'd left out for her.

She coughed loudly and then opened the door.

'Oh hi, Mum,' said Kate, her face flushed and her eyes bright, 'this is Tony, do you remember, I told you about him. He was in my physical rehab group and he just dropped by.'

'So I see,' said the woman, 'hello Tony, nice to meet you.'

'You too,' he said, getting up from the sofa.

He was quite young, early twenties, she thought. Good looking, like a young David Essex.

'Don't get up,' she said, 'I'll make you a both a cup of tea.'

'Oh, thanks,' he said, giving her a smile, and sitting down again.

'Did you have your dinner?' she asked Kate before going into the kitchen.

'Yes, it was really tasty, Mum.'

'Good' she said. She'd left out a cold chicken salad for her, with some buttered bread.

Well, well, well, she thought as she made the tea and put some crisps in a bowl. So Kate had an admirer.

She could certainly do with a bit of romance in her life. He did seem quite young but maybe that was a good thing in view of everything that had happened.

Kate was twenty-seven now and hadn't had a boyfriend for five years. Not since a man she'd been dancing with in a club had asked her and another couple if they wanted to go back to his flat and watch a movie. After about half an hour, the other girl didn't feel well and she and the guy with her, left. The man re-started the film and as he and Kate sat on the sofa watching it, he suddenly leant his body over hers and started to kiss her passionately. Memories of the rape came flooding back and she pushed him off violently, ran into the bathroom and locked the door. She must never let it happen to her again. She realised she was drunk and not in control of herself. Feeling sick and shaking she opened the window and looked out. It didn't seem that high.

The man was banging on the door, telling her not to be stupid, he only wanted a kiss and a cuddle and she could go home now if she wanted, but she wouldn't listen to him. The horror of the rape had filled her head and she just climbed over the sill and jumped.

It was a really bad landing. She broke both her ankles and her right leg in three places with the bones all jammed up into each other. She had to have three operations to try and repair the damage. Sadly they'd all failed and in the end it had been decided that amputation above the knee was the only solution for her right leg.

Kate had told the hospital and the police, that she'd had too much to drink and was only messing about when she fell. It wasn't the fault of the man, she said, it was her, she was just being stupid. She didn't tell them the real reason she'd jumped. About the rape, and the fear that it could happen again. She couldn't face talking about it to strangers, even after all this time.

It changed everything for her, of course.

After the amputation she was finally released from hospital and her mum cared for her at home.

§

Her mother put the tea and a bowl of sugar and some crisps on a tray and took them in to the sitting room.

'Right, now,' she said to Tony, 'tell me all about yourself.'

Chapter Twenty

As the two sisters were discussing the plan for Rachael and George to move back into the old house, their mother came in from the kitchen, looking very pale and clutching her chest.

'Are you alright, Mum?' Rachael and Lorna both said, going over to her.

'I'm sorry girls,' she said, 'I don't feel so good, I've got a really bad pain.'

She sank into a chair and they could see sweat breaking out on her forehead and top lip. She was breathing very unevenly in gasps.

'Oh my God,' said Lorna, 'don't worry Mum, we'll call an ambulance.'

'Where's Dad?' asked Rachael, taking her mother's hand.

'He's in the garden,' she gasped out.

'Dad, Dad,' called Lorna running to the back door, 'come quickly, it's Mum, she's not well.'

'I'm fine,' said her mother, 'don't worry, there's no need to make a fuss, aargh!' she clutched her chest again, 'oh, it's going right through to my back.'

Rachael had got her phone out of her pocket and was dialling 999.

'Please can you come quickly, I think my mother's having a heart attack.'

She then had to give them the details and listen carefully to their instructions before they finally told her they'd be there as soon as they could.

Meanwhile her father had come hurrying in from the garden with Torvill and Dean, leaving muddy footprints from the vegetable plot all over the carpet.

'You alright, love?' he said going straight over to his wife, 'you look a bit of a funny colour,' he knelt down next to her, 'try not to panic, we'll get you sorted.'

'Take your boots off,' she said, breathlessly.

He stroked her hair, clumsily.

'The ambulance will be here soon,' he said, 'they'll set you right.'

It arrived after about twenty minutes. The paramedics worked on her for a short time, then got her onto a stretcher and carried her into the back of the ambulance. Their father got in as well, to travel with her.

'We'll follow on in the car,' said Rachael.

'See you soon Mum,' called Lorna, as the driver was shutting the doors.

As it drove off, they looked at other in silence for a moment.

'Come on' said Rachael, as Lorna's face began to crumble, 'let's go and get a few things together that Mum might need in the hospital.'

She instinctively put her arm round Lorna's shoulder and they went back into the house.

Chapter Twenty-one

Rachael took a deep breath as she and George walked up the stairs to their old front door.

It had been a hell of a week. With her poor mum being rushed off to hospital and the fear that they were going to lose her. Fortunately the doctors were able to treat her quickly and get it under control. They confirmed that she'd had a minor heart attack, but were hopeful that she would make a good recovery. She was still in the ward, waiting for an angiogram, but seemed cheerful and almost back to her usual self.

'I told you it was nothing to worry about,' she told her husband and daughters.

Of course they were all worried sick. They took it in turns to visit her and bring flowers and cards and presents. She and Lorna were concerned about their dad but he seemed to be coping well so far. Rachael had packed up all of her and George's stuff, and put them in the back of her car. She knew that it would be really important that the house was quiet and peaceful when her mum came out of hospital but she was glad that Lorna would still be around to keep an eye on both their parents.

Moving back into her old home was bound to be traumatic. She had picked George up from school and now here they were. She unlocked the door and they went in. She put down the three heavy bags of stuff she'd brought from her parents' house and turned off the alarm. George went straight into the sitting room, and stood looking at the place where his father had been stabbed.

'He's gone,' he said after a moment when she followed him in.

'Yes darling he's gone,' said Rachael coming up and putting her arms round him.

'And he won't be coming back.'

'That's right,' she said kissing the top of his head.

'Because he's dead.'

'Yes.'

'I like the carpet,' he said, 'it looks like a beach.'

He rushed back out into the hall and got down on his hands and knees.

'What are you doing?'   asked Rachael, following him, bemused.

'They've gone too,' he said.

'What have?'

'The three dots. They looked like blood.'

He must have noticed them as they left the house together the morning after the murder. She was amazed how observant he had been, when there was so much mayhem going on. Of course she knew now, that he'd seen some of it happen. She hoped to God he'd get over it alright. What a dreadful thing for a child to see. The police had told her that if he started to show any signs of abnormal behaviour, she should contact them and they would put her touch with a child psychiatrist. She hoped it wouldn't be necessary, but it was good to know what to do, if she was worried about him.

'Well this carpet's been cleaned, darling, so they managed to get rid of the marks, whatever they were.'

'They were blood,' said George, firmly.

'Right,' said Rachael, not knowing how best to respond.

'Shall we go upstairs and have a look at your room,' she went on, changing the subject.

'Yes,' said George, suddenly excited, 'come on, Mummy,' he shouted as he went racing up the stairs. He was thrilled to see all his old toys and immediately got all his plastic dinosaurs out of their box and started standing them all up all over the floor.

Rachael laughed, 'I'll go and get your stuff from down stairs,' she said.

'Alright, Mummy,' he replied, already lost in his own world.

§

Clare had offered to get a baby-sitter for Angus and come round to keep her company on her first night back. What a friend. It made such a difference. They opened a bottle of Merlot and had a take-away pizza. They got the fire going and sat on the sofa watching the flames and talking about life and where it was leading them.

'If you and George can't settle in, you can always come and stay with me and Angus for a bit,' said Clare.

'That's so kind of you, but I think we're going to be alright. The sooner I can get George back into his old routine, the easier it will be for him, I think.'

'And what about you?' Clare asked, 'are you going to be able to cope, after everything that's happened?'

'I'll keep you posted!' said Rachael, finishing the end of her wine.

After Clare had left, Rachael had a long hot bath, checked that George was still asleep and finally braced herself for the hardest part of all. Getting into the double bed, without Michael lying next to her.

It was very strange. The bed seemed so large. She moved the pillows to the centre then turned onto her back with her arms flung out either side. It felt good.

Chapter Twenty-two

Grandad sat by the side of Nana's hospital bed, holding her hand.

'You OK, love?' he asked.

'Oh, I'll get by,' she said.

'You'd better,' said Grandad, 'there's no way I can manage without you, what with all the things that are going on.'

'I know,' said Nana, 'what's the latest?'

'Well, Rachael and George have moved out and gone back home and I must say the house does feel a bit quieter.'

'I shall miss George,' said Nana, 'he's such a funny little chap.'

'I know,' said Grandad, 'but it was getting a bit much for us, wasn't it? Especially with Lorna coming back as well.'

'How's she doing,' asked Nana, 'is she coping better?'

'Well she's moved up into her old room now, so the sitting room's back to normal.'

'Oh good,' said Nana, 'is she still crying all the time?'

'It's easing off a bit. Silly girl, what did she expect, carrying on with Michael like that.'

'She feels awful about it,' said Nana, always quick to defend the more wayward of her two girls.

'I know, but even so,' said Grandad, 'there are some things you just don't do, and sleeping with your sister's husband is one of them. I had a good talk with her about it, last night.'

'Don't be too hard on her,' said Nana, worried. She wished she was at home and could calm things down, like she usually did.

'Don't fret yourself, she's all right,' said Grandad, noticing that Nana's cheeks had become very flushed.

'I'll tell you what,' he went on, changing the subject, 'she makes a damned good spaghetti bolognese.'

Nana laughed.

'I didn't think you were that keen on Italian food' she said, 'you usually want shepherd's pie or bangers and mash.'

'Beggars can't be choosers,' said Grandad, 'and it was very tasty.'

'I'll ask her to give me the recipe when I get back.'

'That's the spirit,' said Grandad.

He couldn't wait for her to come home. He realised how much he missed her. He felt lost without her. They'd been together for so many years and all the little things they did together and took for granted, seemed so precious to him now that she wasn't by his side. He really didn't think he would be able to carry on without her, if she died. He tried not to think about it.

'Oh I must tell you,' Nana said, lowering her voice, 'you see the lady in the middle bed over there?'

Grandad looked over at the frail looking woman, lying back on her pillow and looking as if she was at death's door.

'Yes,' he said.

'Well last night at visiting, all her family were gathered around her bed, just standing there, not talking, and she suddenly sat up and said loudly, 'Oh cheer up, all of you, I've had enough of your long faces.'

'Oh dear,' said Grandad, smiling in spite of himself.

'It was funny,' said Nana, 'they all left soon after.'

'Well, I suppose I'd better be leaving soon, too, in case you get fed up with my face!' he said.

'Don't go,' said Nana. 'It's really nice having you here. Stay a little longer.'

'All right then,' said Grandad, patting her hand, 'but I don't want to tire you out and I should get back to Torvill and Dean before too long, I don't want them to start barking.'

To tell the truth he was feeling really tired himself. The trip to the hospital on the bus took longer than driving over, but the car park fees were so expensive, that it was worth it. His legs really ached while he was waiting for the bus and then it was a fifteen minute walk for him once he was in the hospital, to get up to Marigold Ward which was right at the back on the fifth floor.

'Don't worry about me,' said Nana, smiling at him, 'I'm fine.'

It was so good to see his familiar face when he arrived in the ward, usually clutching some flowers or a magazine. He came every afternoon, Lorna came early evening, most days, after work at the bank, and Rachael would drop by for a visit before picking up George from school. This weekend she was going to bring him with her, to see his Nana.

Nana had told Grandad that the visits from them all made it bearable. She knew she was lucky. The woman in the corner hadn't had a single visitor since she had arrived four days ago.

She leant over and fished out a list from her bedside cabinet.

'Could you be a love and bring these things in for me tomorrow?' she asked, handing it over.

His heart sank. It looked like quite a long list. Lip salve, her blue nightie, two more pairs of pants from her top drawer, a packet of fruit gums, her crossword book from the rack beside the television and few more bits and bobs. Blimey, he thought, he'd have to get Lorna to help him; he'd be bound to bring the wrong things.

'Of course I will' he said, putting it in his pocket.
'I'd ask the girls but they're both so busy, I don't like to bother them,' said Nana.

She'd already given Rachael a plastic bag, with a nightdress, bed socks and some underwear to wash through for her, when she'd come at the start of visiting. She didn't want Grandad to have to deal with those. She was so used to being in control of everything at home and it was strange having to ask for help. It made her feel vulnerable and insecure. She hoped she wouldn't have to stay in the hospital for too long. The staff told her that she would probably have her angiogram in about a week but it might have to be delayed if more urgent cases came in before then. It was as long as a piece of string, she thought.

One of the nurses came into the ward.

'Right, that's it everyone, I'm afraid' she said cheerily, 'time to leave all these lovely ladies in peace.'

Grandad got to his feet, stiffly. He leant over and kissed Nana on the forehead.

'Chin up, Sweetheart,' he said, 'see you tomorrow.'

124

As she watched him walk out of the ward, Nana felt a pang of sadness as she realised how stooped he had become. He was seven years older than her and she'd always thought he would be the first to go. Now she wasn't so sure any more and if she went first, how on earth would he manage?

She gave a sigh, lay back on her pillow, and closed her eyes.

Chapter Twenty-three

The woman watched from further up the street as the silver-haired man, his wife and the two children came out of their house and got into the car. The children looked excited as if they were going somewhere nice.

Perfect, she thought as she saw them drive away, now she would have the house to herself. She wanted to find out everything she could about him. Hopefully have a good snoop in his desk or study and get photos of some of his contacts, people she could threaten to tell if he didn't play ball with her blackmail demands.

She drove to the next turning and drove slowly down it. Sure enough there was a small alleyway that served all the bins at the back of the houses. She parked, and walked down the path until she was behind the man's house. She knew it was his because he had a cockerel weather vane on his roof. Well, he would, wouldn't he, she thought as she gazed up at it.

She tried the back gate but it was locked. She looked around and couldn't see anyone watching, so she climbed onto a big re-cycling bin and deftly jumped over the fence and down the other side. Easy. She made a show of looking in the bushes and behind the shed. If anyone questioned her, she would say she had lost her cat and thought she heard a miaow coming from the garden. She made her way up to the back door. Locked. She looked round to see if there was a spare key under a rock.

She noticed a small stone Buddha against the wall and tipped it gently to one side. Eureka! There was a key, lying there, waiting for her. The Buddha looked very peaceful and had his eyes closed. Fallen asleep on the job, matey, she thought as she picked it up.

She let herself into the kitchen and closed the door carefully behind her. She stood stock still and listened. Silence. No alarm sounding; they must have forgotten to set it, if they had one. She was wearing her soft soled shoes and she crept quietly into the hall. There were some letters on the small table. Dr Peter Carstairs. A doctor! Perfect! He had no business dallying with a young woman who wasn't his wife. Maybe she was even a patient! Very strong pressure point, that would be.

She went into the living room and looked around. All very tasteful and elegant, but no sign of a desk. How people lived their lives with so little clutter, she never knew.

She looked in at another open door that led to a dining room. The table all laid with silver and glasses as if they were about to host a dinner-party or something. There was a cabinet with bottles of alcohol on it and she was tempted to go and have a swig, but thought better of it. Keep your mind on the job, dearie, she told herself.

He's got to have a study, she thought, being a doctor and all. It must be upstairs.

She went up to the top landing and saw a door with a hand-painted notice on it saying Gone Fishing. Mmm, what are you hoping to catch Dr Carstairs she thought as she turned the handle! Yes, she was right, it was his study. She went in, closing the door behind her, then crossed over to the desk and started to look through his paperwork. It was very untidy. I'm glad you're not my doctor, she thought. She found a couple of useful letters and took photos of them on her smart phone then crossed over to his computer, knocking an empty mug off the table as she sat down in the swivel chair. Damn. Luckily it didn't break. She picked it up and put it back.

Suddenly, the door burst open and a tall young man, holding a baseball bat, stood in the doorway.

'Who the hell are you?' he shouted at her.

He only looked about eighteen, but well built, with tousled hair. He was wearing a T-shirt, boxers and a pair of red, loose-knit socks. He looked as if he'd just got out of bed.

The woman jumped to her feet.

'I'm here to see Doctor Carstairs,' she said, thinking quickly and trying to sound as confident as she could.

'I don't believe you,' he said, 'my father never sees his patients at home.'

Of course. It was the man's son. Probably by his first marriage, she thought. Why had she never considered that possibility? She needed to up her game.

'Phone your father if you don't believe me,' she said, noticing that he didn't have his phone with him.

'How did you get in?' he asked, taking a step towards her.

'The door was open,' she said, trying to work out how to get past him and out of the house. She wasn't happy about the baseball bat. They can do a fair amount of damage, she thought.

'It so wasn't,' he said, taking another step towards her and raising the bat, 'you'd better tell me what you're doing here or I'll hit you with this.'

'Oh, here's your father now!' she said, looking beyond him to the landing.

As he turned to look, she raced past him and headed for the stairs.

'Oh no, you don't,' he shouted, following her out onto the landing, 'I'm calling the police.'

He tried to grab hold of her but his red knitted socks slipped on the polished wooden landing and he plummeted full length down the stairs, ending with a terrible crash on the tiled hall floor. The baseball bat flying out of his hand and clattering down after him.

She stopped short, shocked by the noise, waited a moment and then went slowly down the stairs towards him. Not too quickly, in case he suddenly jumped up and grabbed her. No chance of that she realised as she took in the contorted angle of his head. He must have broken his neck, she thought. Oh shit, what now? His limbs were all over the place as well and there was no movement. No sound. Just a big silent crumpled mess, with no sign of life. He was dead.

Oh God, it was happening again. First Kate's rapist and now this young lad.

She heard a car pulling up in the road outside and realised that she had to get out of the house as quickly as possible. If she was found here she could be accused of his murder. They'd never believe it was an accident.

She ran back into the kitchen and went out locking the door behind her and replacing the key under the Buddha. She let herself out through the back gate; she wouldn't be able to bolt it again, but someone could easily have forgotten to do it, no-one could ever be sure.

She hurried back to her car and got in. She drove straight off and   after about five minutes, pulled in to a quiet road. She turned the engine off and took some deep breaths trying to calm herself down and think things through.

Her plan had been to find info about the man and take photos of anything that could be useful in the blackmail scam. Well, she could kiss goodbye to that idea now, she thought. Damn. She had intended to leave everything undisturbed so no-one would even know she had been there.

Still, assuming the lad was dead and she was pretty sure he was, there was no reason for anyone to suspect anything other than a tragic accident.

The only problem was the baseball bat. She shouldn't have left it there, but she was panicking and trying to get out of the house quickly. Hopefully it would be assumed that he'd heard a suspicious noise downstairs and was on his way down to investigate, when he slipped.

She was in the clear, she thought. Anyway, it actually was an accident. Him falling down the stairs wasn't her fault, so there was no point in beating herself up about it. She felt sad about him though, he was nice-looking lad. He would have been a nice match for her Kate.

She must never tell Kate what had just happened, she thought.

She'd learnt long ago that nobody is capable of keeping a secret for ever.

Chapter Twenty-four

The child was in his room, deeply involved in a game.
Mummy was downstairs on the phone to Angus' mummy.
They always talked for ages and it was so boring. He'd found
a packet of custard creams and taken them upstairs to look for
something to do while he ate them. It was Saturday and it was
raining, so they wouldn't be going out. But now he'd got all
his dinosaurs out of the box and he sat on the floor and stood
them up, on one side of the room. They looked like an army.

They were the baddies.

On the other side were all his soft toys.

They were the goodies.

They were going to fight each other!

Eeyore was going to be Mummy and fight the biggest
dinosaur, because she was very brave.

Mummy would win easily because she had a special invisible
sword. She whacked it over the head of the big scary dinosaur.
He fell over straight away and George threw him into the box.

'Hooray', he said, and sat Eeyore up on his pillow. The winner.

Next came Daddy. But was he a goody or a baddy? He wasn't sure. He picked up his green hippo and then changed his mind. No, Daddy was a baddy because he'd hurt Mummy and made her sad. He chose an angry looking dinosaur with lots of black and green spikes. That was going to be Daddy.

But who was he going to fight?

It had to be 'the lady'.

He looked at his Spider-Man. Yes. He could be her. But who should win? They fought a long battle, with George making fierce noises for both of them. Eventually Spider-Man won and the green dinosaur fell to the floor with a loud roar. It was only fair, because even though 'the lady' had stabbed Daddy, he had been hurting her and making her cry, like he did with Mummy.

He threw Daddy into the box.

He put Spider-Man right at the end of the bed. Although she was a winner he didn't really want 'the lady' on his pillow.

He found a white polar bear to be Nana. She only had to fight the smallest little dinosaur, because she wasn't very strong. She was back home from the hospital, and had to rest a lot and keep quiet. He and Mummy had been to see her and she looked fine. She said the doctors had mended her and she'd bought him a little pot of bubbles, from the hospital shop. He loved Nana.

She won the fight easily just by blowing bubbles at the little dinosaur, who fell over at once.

George laughed as he put the white polar bear on his pillow.

'Well done Nana,' he said.

He threw the tiny dinosaur up into the air and it landed in the box.

'Goal' he shouted triumphantly.

Next was Grandad. Easy. He picked up Heffalump and stood it in front of the dinosaur with the longest tail. Wham, bang, it tried to whip Grandad with his tail, but Grandad just laughed and jumped on him, squashing him to the ground.

Into the box it went and onto the pillow went Heffalump.

The next fight was the best of all.

He chose Stretch Armstrong to be Angus and stood him in front of *three* scary dinosaurs. Ready steady go. They all rushed at him, but Stretch pulled his muscly arms as far wide as they would go and wrapped them round all three of the bullies and rolled around with them. They tried to biff him but Stretch wound his legs round them as well and tied them into a knot so they couldn't escape.

'Yes, go on Angus, you're winning!' shouted George.

In the end Stretch got so excited he jumped into the box with them and George had to untie his legs and untangle his arms before getting him out and putting him on the pillow with the other winners.

'Good one, Angus,' he said, 'that'll show them.'

He suddenly heard Mummy calling from downstairs.

'Tea's ready George, come on down.'

'Coming Mummy,' he called, looking at the empty biscuit wrapper. He seemed to have eaten them all. Never mind, he was still hungry.

He raced downstairs, leaving the rest of the goodies and baddies all over the floor. They'd just have to sort it out between themselves.

Chapter Twenty-five

The Coroner had released Michael's body and finally it was the day of the funeral.

Rachael felt George was too young to be there, that it would only upset and confuse him. Luckily, Clare had offered to collect him from school and take him back to have tea with Angus.

As she sat in the front pew, Rachael looked past her parents, at Lorna, who was crying quietly. There was no sign of Chris by her side of course. He and Michael had never got on anyway. Rachael wondered if Chris had suspected something going on between them, long before it all came out into the open.

She turned her head and looked across to the other side of the church. Michael's mother and sister were sitting next to each other, both sniffing into hankies. They had flown in from Canada the day before. Cold and frosty towards her as always, giving the impression that they never thought her worthy of being Michael's wife. His father had died of a heart attack ten years ago and he had a brother who lived in England but had chosen not to come. Sibling rivalry had caused a falling out between them years ago and they had never spoken since.

One row back, were some of his colleagues from the health club, and a couple of girls who worked in the pool area. They were both in tears. He had been able to charm the birds off the trees when he wanted to.

Rachael wasn't crying.

The rest of the church was only half full. Some of the people she recognised, some she didn't. She and Michael hadn't had many friends and most of her own had fallen by the wayside after her marriage. He'd somehow always managed to make them feel unwelcome.

She felt the hairs on the back of her neck tingling. She couldn't shake off the feeling that somewhere amongst the people present, could be Michael's killer.

When she arrived, she had seen there were some press outside, waiting to take photos of the mourners. She wondered if the police had one of their own men amongst them, to get a picture of everyone who attended.

She had also noticed the Chief Inspector and the Detective Inspector as she entered the church, both standing quietly at the back, dressed in sombre clothes and taking in every movement and reaction of the congregation.

Was the woman here? And why had she killed him?

She was aware of a sudden hush and realised that the coffin was being carried down the aisle to its resting point at the front of the church. She closed her eyes. Her mother took her hand and gave it a small squeeze.

As the vicar stepped up to talk to the congregation, she looked at the coffin in disbelief. It didn't seem possible that Michael's body was inside it, lying there unable to speak, move or breathe. Actually dead. She felt dizzy as the short service continued. It was obvious from the vicar's address that he had not known Michael. He did his best, but could have been talking about any man in his fifties who had died an unfortunate and violent death. His words began to drift past her and she found it hard to take in what he was saying.

A co-director of the health club said a few words about Michael, and a lady from the church, who had an exceptionally quiet voice, read a passage from the bible that no one could hear.

Finally the service ended.

Solemnly, the congregation followed the coffin as it was carried from the church. As they walked through the graveyard to the freshly dug grave, Rachael approached Michael's mother and sister.

'I'm sorry George isn't here to meet you,' she said, 'but I felt he was too young to come.'

'Yes well, we were hoping to meet him of course,' said Michael's mother, not looking her in the eye.

'Perhaps we could arrange for you to visit us in the next few days,' said Rachael.

'Unfortunately that won't be possible,' Michael's mother replied, 'we fly to Germany tomorrow morning to visit my brother.'

'And after that we fly home to Canada,' said Michael's sister, dismissively.

Michael's mother had never shown any interest in George. Had never sent him cards or presents for Christmas or birthdays.

'My family don't do presents,' Michael had said, 'never have, never will.'

How sad, Rachael had thought. She'd sent some photos of George to Canada when he was about three months old and eventually got a reply from Michael's mother.

'Dear Rachael, thank you for sending the photos of George. I must say he doesn't look anything like Michael when he was a baby. He does seem to have very dark hair.'

Nothing about how sweet he looked, or how they couldn't wait to meet him. Rachael had the distinct impression that they didn't believe the baby was Michael's. What a dysfunctional family, she thought. Thank God they lived in Canada.

'Oh well, never mind,' she said, as they all walked through the graveyard, their heels snagging in the wet grass, 'maybe next time you're over here.'

'Yes, maybe next time,' said Michael's mother, pulling her coat around her, 'it's very cold here isn't it?' she said grumpily.

'Yes, I'm so sorry,' said Rachael.

How ridiculous, she thought. I'm apologising for the bad weather.

'Excuse me,' she said to them, 'I must join my parents.'
She hurried forward and caught up with her mother and father.

'Alright love?' asked her mother.

'You're doing grand,' her father said, putting his arm round her shoulder.
She felt so grateful for their warmth and understanding. Maybe coming from such a tricky family went a long way to explain Michael's problems.

As they were approaching the grave, she caught sight of an older woman with a girl in a wheelchair on the other side of the graveyard. They seemed to be watching the line of mourners as they walked slowly along.

Poor things, thought Rachael. It's probably taking them back to a sad and traumatic time in their own lives.

Chapter Twenty-six

Five days later, Rachael got a call from the murder team.

'Just to keep you up to date,' the Chief Inspector, said, 'we've had a breakthrough concerning the woman who murdered your husband.'

'Oh, right,' said Rachael, her pulse speeding up, 'what have you found?'

'A young man, in Guildford, discovered a woman had broken into his house and was in his father's study, looking through his papers. She claimed to be waiting to see Dr Peter Carstairs, the young man's father. She then made a break for it, there was a tussle and he fell, or was pushed, down the flight of stairs, knocking himself out and breaking a leg and one of his wrists. When he came round, she had gone. Fortunately his father returned home shortly afterwards, and was able to attend to his son at once and call an ambulance.'

'So how is this connected to my husband's death?' Rachael asked, shaken by the thought that Michael's murderer might be revealed. She almost didn't want to know. She just wanted it all to go away.

'There was no sign of a forced entry but the woman's fingerprints were on the back door handle and also on the stair bannisters and in the study.'

'Yes?' said Rachael, breathlessly.

'They are a perfect match for the prints we found in your house on the day of your husband's murder.'

'Oh my God,' said Rachael, sinking onto a chair, 'so you've found her?'

'Well not yet, but we are on our way,' the Chief Inspector said.

'The other thing,' he went on, 'is that the young man was able to give us an excellent description of what she looked like, and it tallies exactly with what your son George told us.'

'I see,' said Rachael, wondering what was coming next.

'I wanted to let you know,' the Chief Inspector said, 'that we will be showing an E-FIT picture of her in 'Crime Catch-up' this evening, with a request that anyone who knows who this woman is, should get in touch with the police at the first possible opportunity, in order to help with their enquiries concerning your husband's murder.'

'Right,' said Rachael shakily, 'well thank you for letting me know.'

'Also, I need to ask if you have ever had any contact with this Dr Peter Carstairs, the young man's father?' he asked.

'No. I've never heard of him,' said Rachael, defensively, suddenly feeling under suspicion.

'That's fine, don't worry,' said the Chief Inspector, 'but we may need to talk to you again about him, in case you are able to find any link between him and your husband. If you think of any possible reason why your husband might have contacted him, do get in touch with us immediately.'

'Yes, of course,' said Rachael, ' but I don't think….'

'We'll leave it there for now,' the Chief Inspector went on, 'of course we'll keep you informed of any further developments.'

'Thank you,' said Rachael.

'Not at all,' he said, and ended the call.

Rachel sat in silence for a few minutes. None of this made any sense to her. Who was this woman? What was she doing in the Doctor's house? Come to that, what had she been doing in *her* house. Was she a serial killer? Had she pushed the young man down the stairs? And was she on her way to the kitchen to grab a knife and finish him off, when she heard his father returning and made her escape?

Dr Peter Carstairs. She racked her brains. Nothing. Why would Michael have ever contacted him and about what?

She went and made herself a cup of tea and then sat down and phoned Clare.

Thank God she had a friend to talk to.

Chapter Twenty-seven

The woman was in the kitchen watching the small television while she made supper. 'Crime Catch-up' came on. Good.

She always watched the programme, hoping to learn how the investigation was going into Michael Stanhope's murder. They didn't seem to be making much progress, so far. Hopefully the case would eventually go cold and she wouldn't have to worry.

There were a couple of items concerning two burglaries and then suddenly, to her horror, there was a large E-FIT picture of herself, staring back at her. Not a very good one thankfully, but too close for comfort.

She went into an immediate state of shock, letting the gravy boil over, and hardly able to take in the voice of the presenter.

'If anyone recognises this woman, please contact the police on the number below, to help with enquiries concerning the murder three months ago of Michael Stanhope director of 'Out There Health Clubs,' he was saying, *'she is also wanted in connection with a break-in and possible attempted murder at a doctor's house in .....'*

She quickly switched the television off and went and looked into the sitting room. Thank goodness Kate and her new boyfriend, Tony, were sitting on the sofa holding hands. Her wheelchair was pushed to the side of the room and they were listening to music, both with their eyes closed.

Thank God, they hadn't seen it.

She went back into the kitchen, cleaned up the gravy and sank onto the stool.

Shit. How the hell had they got her description?

There was only one possible answer. The young lad with the baseball bat, Dr Carstairs' son, must still be alive. She had been so sure he was dead but he must have regained consciousness after she'd left. There had been nothing on the news about it. Why the delay? Maybe he had been in a coma, then come round and told the police what had happened. But what had he told them? Did he say he fell down the stairs by accident or did he say she pushed him? He must have, if she was wanted for attempted murder. She felt a cold sense of fear trickling through her. This was turning ugly. And how had they linked the description he gave, with the stabbing of Michael Stanhope?

The fingerprints.

Of course, the sodding fingerprints would be a match. How could she have been so careless. Well, she hadn't known the son would be there. Her plan had been just to have a snoop round and no-one would have been any the wiser but she should have worn gloves anyway, just in case.

Still, the police didn't know who she was. No-one had come round enquiring about her and if she kept her head down and no-one recognised her from the E-FIT she might still get away with it.

She cursed the fact that she and Kate had gone to watch the funeral. How stupid was that? But she didn't think anyone had noticed them, they were a fair distance away. Well at least she had been wearing a headscarf and glasses. Kate had wanted so badly to finally see the bastard lowered into the ground. And she herself felt a compulsion to see it too. To say farewell to the man she had killed on behalf of her daughter. With the horror of it came a strange thrill of power that she had actually managed to make him pay for his actions.

They had found out the day and place of the funeral and decided to go for it. Of course, Kate had no idea that it had been her own mother who had killed him. She must never know, she might let something slip to someone by mistake. She herself, would never confide in a soul. Her life was at stake. Now more than ever.

The next thing she must do is to change her appearance, in case they showed the E-FIT again in a later programme.

That night as she was helping Kate into bed, she pulled the duvet up and gave an unexpected little laugh.

'Guess what?' she said, 'I've had a brilliant idea.'

'What?' asked Kate, intrigued.

'Tomorrow, let's do a 'make-over' for both of us. Dye our hair, change our make-up, nail varnish, pedicure, the lot.'

'That's a great idea, Mum,' said Kate, who got really bored, spending so much time just sitting around in her chair.
'Then we can sort through our clothes and try and work out some fresh outfits,' the woman went on, 'we always seem to be wearing the same old things. We can go online and treat ourselves. Give ourselves a totally new look.'

Chapter Twenty-eight

Rachael was sitting on the sofa watching 'Crime Catch-up' with a large glass of Merlot. She'd managed to get George into bed early so she could give the programme her full attention. She was also recording it in case she wanted to play it back again later.

The face of a woman suddenly filled the screen.

'If anyone recognises this person, please contact the police on the number below, to help with enquiries concerning the murder three months ago of Michael Stanhope, director of 'Out There Health Clubs,' he was saying, *'she is also wanted in connection with a break-in and possible attempted murder at a doctor's house in Guildford.'*

Rachael stared at the picture. George was right, she did look like Miss Harold, his head mistress. A bit scary, dark hair pulled back in a bun. Dark eyes in a heavy-set face. Rachael was convinced that she had never met her, she would have remembered. She didn't look at all like the kind of woman that Michael would have fancied. She was too old for a start, he'd liked them young and slim. So what was the connection? Why had she killed him in such a violent attack? And why did she cut his wrists as well as stabbing him? What did that mean? There must have been a reason. It wasn't a robbery gone wrong. No forced entry and nothing had been taken, apart from the eight inch knife which was missing from the set. The police believed it was the murder weapon. Apparently, the serrated edge would correspond with Michael's wounds.

The programme showed the photo of her and George on the beach again and also a short video of Michael at a work presentation 'do'. It was weird to see him moving and talking with his easy charm. He looked such a nice kind man. She shuddered.

The face of the woman came back on the screen with numbers to phone or text with any information.

Her mobile rang. It was Clare.

'Bloody hell Rachael, I wouldn't want to meet her on a dark night,' she said.

Rachael couldn't help laughing, even though the sight of the woman made her feel sick to her stomach.

'Did you recognise her at all?' asked Clare.

'No, I'm sure I've never met her,' said Rachael.

'They were saying that she's also wanted in connection with another murder!'

'Yes, I know,' said Rachael, shakily, 'what's that all about? Do you think she's a serial killer? I can't help thinking that she might come back for me and George.'

'Oh, you poor thing,' Clare said, 'well look, try not to panic; you've got new locks, and a special alarm system now haven't you? I'm sure you don't need to worry. It would be too risky for her to return to the same place.'

'Maybe... I don't know,' said Rachael taking another swig of wine, 'anyway, I put the house on the market today. I just know I have to leave as soon as possible. I thought I could hack it, coming back here, but I really can't.'

'I think that's the right thing to do,' said Clare, 'look I'm going to have to go, Angus is fussing. Do you want to come round with George for a bit, if you're feeling freaked out?'

'No, it's OK he's asleep. I'll be fine, don't worry about me.'

'Alright, if you're sure,' said Clare.

'Yes, really, but thanks anyway.'

'See you at school in the morning, then.'

'Yeah, bye now,' said Rachael turning her phone off.

She was about to go and check on George, when the doorbell rang.

Who the hell was this? She wasn't expecting anyone. No-one came to the house in the evening just out of the blue.

The woman?

She felt a sudden terror and a chill ran through her. Her heart started racing and she felt sick. She went to the window and looked out, but the front porch blocked the view and she couldn't see anyone.

The bell rang again.

She forced herself to go towards the front door to look through the peep-hole. If she saw it was her, she'd call the police straight away and lock herself and George in her bedroom until they came.

Whoever it was, started banging on the door with their fist. She took a deep breath and slowly lifted the shutter on the peep-hole and looked through…

Chapter Twenty-nine

She felt a sudden terror and a chill ran through her. Her heart started racing... she went to the window and looked out, but the front porch blocked the view and she couldn't see anyone

'Come on Kate, it's 'Makeover Day'! We're going to have such a good time,' the woman said cheerily to her daughter when she came back from the supermarket. She was wearing her hair down for once, falling messily about her face, trying to conceal her appearance before anyone recognised her from the picture on 'Crime Catch-up'.

'What's brought all this on?' asked Kate, warily. This was very unlike her Mum.

'It's time for a change, that's all. Right, we'll do you first,' her mother said, coming behind Kate's wheelchair and running her hands through the long brown hair.

'What do you fancy. Shall we cut it short or just add highlights? Or we could give it a gentle perm if you like, just to give it a bit of body.'

Kate's face brightened. Although she was a bit alarmed at the sudden turn of events, she'd wanted curly hair for ages.

'A perm would be great,' she said, 'can you do it, really?'

'Course I can, easy-peasy,' the woman said, fishing out a packet from her shopping bag and waving it in front of Kate, 'but first, I want you to cut me a fringe.'

She knelt down in front of her and handed her a pair of scissors.

'*Mum*!' Kate exclaimed, 'you've never had a fringe!'

'I know,' said the woman, laughing, 'isn't it fun!'

She was in a very odd mood, thought Kate, feeling a bit anxious.

She combed her mother's hair over her face and carefully cut a fringe for her. Before her accident she'd spent a summer assisting in a local hair salon so she had a rough idea of what to do.

'Great,' said her mother without even looking at it in the mirror, 'now cut me a short bob.'

'Mum!!!' said Kate, thinking her mother was losing her senses.

'Just do it,' said the woman, firmly, 'I've had the same hairstyle for so many years – it's time I had a change.'

'You'd better wash it first, Mum.'

'No just cut it dry. It'll be fine.'

Mid-life crisis, Kate thought to herself. Best to humour her, she could get a bit tricky if you challenged her about things.

'OK, here goes,' she said. She leant forward and cut it as best she could.

'Hurry up, my knees are killing me,' the woman said.

'Well, turn round so I can do the back,' Kate said, brushing some of the hair off her lap.

The woman swivelled round and felt a pang as she saw the cut-offs on the floor. What the hell was she doing? Was this really going to change anything?

'Now back to face me,' said Kate, really getting into it, beginning to feel quite pleased with her handiwork.

'Oh, it makes you look so different!' she said, as she looked at the total effect, 'much younger. I really like it. Go and have a look.'

The woman got up, and looked in the mirror above the fire-place.

'Fantastic,' she said. She hated it. Oh well, it was a start.

'Now you,' she said wheeling Kate into the bathroom, 'you read out the instructions and I'll do it for you.'

'Do you want to clear up the hair in the sitting room first?' Kate asked her.

'No, no, I'll do it later,' said the woman, impatiently, not wanting to look at her long dark hair all over the floor.

'OK, please yourself,' said Kate. She hoped her Mum wasn't having a nervous breakdown or something. She seemed to be either high as a kite or really depressed these days. It was very hard to live with.

They followed the instructions carefully and while the perm was setting, the woman got out the pack of lightener and started to work it into her own newly short hair.

'Mum!' shouted Kate, 'you're not going blonde as well are you?'

'Why not?' her mother answered, defiantly, 'in for a penny in for a pound.'

'Quite a few pounds, if you ask me,' replied Kate.

'Well I didn't ask you, so there you are,' her mother retorted.

Oh shit, I'm not happy with all this, thought Kate. She'd better not mess up my perm and leave me a frizzy mess.

'Tomorrow,' the woman said, 'we'll do our nails. What colour do you want?'

'Black,' said Kate, waiting for her to hit the roof.

'Lovely,' said the woman distractedly, looking at her reflection in the mirror, 'and I need to pop down to the chemist's later and get some reading glasses,' she went on.

'But your sight's fine, Mum,' Kate said, surprised.

'Not as good as I make out,' said the woman, 'oh, quick let's rinse that off,' she went on, changing the subject. She turned Kate's wheelchair round and leant her head back over the sink.

§

By the end of the day they were both thrilled with the changes they had made. Although for different reasons.

Kate had fallen in love with her curly hair and put on full make-up plus the false eyelashes that her mother had bought for her. She wanted to wow Tony when he came round that evening.

By contrast, the woman wore no make-up for the first time in ages and was satisfied that with her new glasses, no-one would make the connection with the E-FIT picture of her. She thought it likely that they'd show it again, so it was good to have changed her appearance quickly, just in case. She hoped no-one locally had been watching. Maybe she and Kate should move. They'd done it often enough over the years for various reasons and the flat was only rented. They could always do a mid-night flit.

The only problem would be Tony, Kate's boyfriend.

She was going to have to do something about him.

Chapter Thirty

'She's being sick again,' said Nana, as they lay in bed drinking their cup of tea.'

'I know,' said Grandad.

It was their morning ritual. The teas-made alarm went off, the water bubbled and boiled and hey presto there was the first cuppa of the day.

They could hear Lorna retching in the bathroom even though she was running the shower to try and cover the noise.

'Its been going on for two weeks now,' said Nana.

'Have you asked her about it?' said Grandad.

'Yes, of course I have. She just says she's got a stomach bug,' said Nana.

'Perhaps she has,' said Grandad, uncertainly, his face a map of worried lines.

'Oh don't be silly,' said Nana, 'we both know what's going on. She's pregnant, isn't she?'

'That's going to put the cat among the pigeons,' said Grandad.

'Yes, it really is,' said Nana, putting her cup on the bedside table and wiping some spilt tea off her chest.

'Do you think it's Chris's?' asked Grandad.

Nana shrugged her shoulders.

'Surely to God it couldn't be Michael's could it?'

'Could be either of them,' said Nana.

'Oh, Lord,' said Grandad, pulling the bedclothes back and heaving himself out of bed, 'I've got to go to the loo.'

'Well, wait till she's finished,' said Nana, pulling the duvet back round her.

'I can't. I've got to go now,' said Grandad, heading for the door.

They heard the shower turn off and Lorna going back into her room.

'All clear,' said Grandad, going out onto the landing.

Nana leant back and closed her eyes. Poor Lorna. What a mess. Her heart ached with the sadness of it all. She had to talk to Lorna again and tell her that they knew. Whoever the father was, it was her grandchild they were talking about. She hoped that, whatever the outcome, Lorna would decide to keep the baby. She'd never forgive herself if she decided to go for an abortion. It would haunt her through the years and she was fragile enough as it was.

A few minutes later, Grandad stumbled back into the room and got back into bed.

'Lets have another cup of tea,' he said. He looked at Nana and caught her wiping away a tear.

'Come on love,' he said, putting his hand on her shoulder, 'it'll be alright. It'll sort itself out, don't worry.'

'Once the baby's born they could have a DNA test to see if it was Chris's', said Nana, 'if it is, maybe Chris could forgive her and they could get back together and bring up the baby and be a proper family.'

'Maybe,' said Grandad, doubtfully, 'you never know.'

'And what about Rachael?' said Nana, 'poor Rachael, what's this going to do to her?'

'Don't say anything to her yet,' said Grandad, 'let's discuss it with Lorna first.'

'Alright,' said Nana, 'I'll talk to her this morning.'

She closed her eyes again. The thing was, even if it was Michael's child it would still be their grandchild. She loved little George to bits and she would love him to have a brother or sister or even a half-brother or half-sister. He was an only child and she worried sometimes that he was missing out on the fun of a bigger family. But with Michael now gone and Lorna and Chris separated, that seemed less and less likely.

But if it was Michael's then why should Chris forgive Lorna and bring up the child as his own; a constant reminder of her infidelity?

If he wouldn't take her back, what then? Lorna would be a single mother with no viable means of support. The thought of having Lorna and the baby living with her and Grandad, was a daunting prospect. As they got older, it was all they could do to keep themselves afloat. What with the increasing numbers of aches and pains, and her heart attack and Grandad's varicose veins and dizzy spells.

The door opened and Lorna popped her head round.

'Morning you two,' she said, 'I'm just off for a bike ride.'

She rushed out and they heard her running down stairs.

Nana raised her eyebrows at Grandad.

'Oh Lord,' she said.

Chapter Thirty-one

Rachael peered through the peephole, her heart racing.

Oh, my God, it was Chris. Lorna's husband. What the hell was he doing here?

She opened the door and let him in.

'Chris, you frightened the life out of me. Come on in.'

She looked beyond him in case there was anyone else out there about to push their way into the hall, then closed the front door firmly. Her nerves were all over the place after seeing the woman on TV, and she made a conscious effort to slow her breathing and calm herself down.

As Chris went into the sitting room in front of her, she thought he looked very changed. She hadn't seen him since he had thrown Lorna out and he had lost weight and was looking somehow scruffy. She also suspected that he'd been drinking.

'Before I say anything else,' Chris began, sitting on the sofa and leaning forward, elbows on his knees, twisting his hands together, 'I have to ask, did you know that Lorna and Michael were sleeping together? Did everyone know? Was I the only one who was kept in the dark?'

Oh God, thought Rachael, he's going to break down. He was sweating, looking very flushed and a bit manic.

'No, of course I didn't know,' she answered quickly, 'I had no idea. I still can't believe it.'

'Neither can I,' he said, rubbing the back of his neck, 'how could she, with such a pompous prick. Oh hell, I'm sorry, he was your husband, I shouldn't have said that.'

'It's OK, Chris,' she said, 'look can I make you a coffee or something?'

'I'd love a whisky,' he said, 'neat, no water.'

'Shaken not stirred,' she said.

She thought she saw a glimmer of a smile, which looked a bit better. He was definitely in an odd state, though. So unlike the self-contained, well turned out Chris she knew.

'Right,' she said, going over to the drinks cabinet and pouring him one, wondering where all this was heading.

'How's work?' she asked, handing him the glass.

'I've left,' he said, throwing back the drink, 'I've chucked it in. I never much liked it there anyway.'

Oh shit, thought Rachael, this is not good.

'Actually,' he went on, 'they asked me to leave. I've not been coping well since Lorna's gone,' his voice started to break, 'we had everything, you know and now she's ruined it all. I don't think I can ever forgive her. We had so many plans for the future, how could she have done it.'

He put his head in his hands and started sobbing.

Rachael took a deep breath and tried to decide how best to cope with this. She'd never found it easy watching men cry.

'Well, none of us are perfect, Chris,' she said, after a moment, putting her hand on his shoulder, 'I know Lorna feels terrible about it all. Maybe there'll come a time when you can get back together and try and move on. It won't be easy, but it might be possible.'

'I don't think that's likely, not after what I'm going to tell you.'

Rachael felt a chill run through her.

'What do mean?' she said.

'I've done something really stupid.'

'Tell me,' she said, sinking down onto the edge of armchair. She didn't think she could cope with any more dramas.

'OK, here goes,' he said sniffing and wiping his face on his sleeve, 'I am so sorry, Rachael, this is the last thing you need.'

'What is it. What on earth have you done?'

'Two nights ago I went out for a drink with a couple of old friends, we all got plastered and by the end of the evening I found myself telling them all about Michael's murder and the fact that Lorna had been sleeping with him - with her own brother-in-law!' he added bitterly, 'I was drunk,' he went on, 'and I probably embellished the story a bit, about what she was like in bed and how I threw her out and so on.'

Where was this leading, thought Rachael. Horrible to think of him talking about Lorna like that, but not unexpected in view of everything.

'Anyway,' he went on, '...look can I have another drink?' he said, interrupting himself.

'Finish the story first,' said Rachael.

'Well, I got a call this afternoon from a guy who'd been sitting at the bar. He's a journalist apparently and he recorded the entire conversation on his phone.'

Rachael's heart sank.

'Well what's he going to do with it?' she asked.

'I'm really sorry, Rachael, but the whole thing's going to be splashed all over the papers tomorrow. They've managed to get all sorts of photos of Michael, and Lorna, and you and George and me. God knows where they've got them from. An awful one they've found of Lorna in a sexy fancy dress outfit ...'

Rachael closed her eyes and put her hand over her mouth. What a nightmare.

'The thing is,' Chris went on, 'the press are going to be coming round here as soon as the story breaks, wanting comments and interviews and taking photos of you and George and everything and I think you should go away for a bit until it's all died down. And can you let your parents know, so they're prepared if the press suddenly turn up at their house. Is Lorna still staying with them, by the way?'

'Yes she is, for the moment,' said Rachael, 'look I think you'd better go now, Chris.'

She needed him to leave so she could process this news on her own.

'I'm so sorry,' said Chris, 'I feel really bad about this.'

'Don't beat yourself up about it,' said Rachael, 'it's done now and you've been through a tough time.'

Chris looked at her and nodded; grateful for her understanding.

'Thanks,' he said, as they started moving towards the door.

§

The child heard them coming towards the hall and raced back upstairs as quickly as he could. He'd been woken up by the banging on the door and looked through the bannisters to see who it was. It was Uncle Chris. He was a bit worried that

Uncle Chris might stab Mummy in the stomach. He'd crept downstairs and peeped through the crack in the door. Why was Uncle Chris crying? He didn't like that. He couldn't understand everything they were saying. Why did it matter if Lorna had been sleeping with Daddy? He and Mummy slept together sometimes. Did it mean he and Mummy would have to go away again? Was it his fault? Was it something he'd done?

He ran back into his room and got into bed.

He pulled the duvet over his head.

Chapter Thirty-two

Chris was right.

The press were outside Rachael's front door, first thing the following morning.

She hurried George past them to get to the car, ignoring all the questions and flashing cameras. Luckily she'd packed a case for them both and put it in the boot the night before. She'd already spoken to Clare, who had suggested they come and stay with her for a few days.

The voices followed them.

'Did you know what your sister was up to with your husband?'

'Does your sister have anything to do with your husband's murder?'

'Has your brother-in law been cleared by the police?'

'Can you ever forgive her?'

The questions went on and on.

'What did they all want, Mummy?' George asked, as she drove him to school.

'Oh they're just being silly, George, don't take any notice,' she said, checking in her mirror to make sure they weren't being followed.

'Are we really going to go and stay with Angus?' he asked, excitedly.

'Yes, just for a bit,' she said, 'I'm really looking forward to it, aren't you?'

'Yes,' said George, 'he's got bunk beds and everything!'

After she'd dropped him off at school, she linked up with Clare.

'This is so kind of you,' Rachael said, 'it was a nightmare at home this morning, the press were all waiting outside the front door. They're like a pack of hyenas.'

'It must be horrible for you,' said Clare, 'anyway, don't worry you can stay as long as you need.'

'Thanks,' said Rachael, 'I suppose I should go and get the papers and see what they've said.'

'Well let's go back and have a cup of coffee and then we can have a look on-line,' said Clare.

'That's a good idea,' said Rachael thankfully. She needed to know the worst and just hoped it wasn't all too sordid.

It was, of course. They'd made a meal out of it all, with big photos of her and Michael, one of Lorna in a dominatrix outfit with a whip, and lots of veiled insinuations as to what might have happened.

'Well, it's done now,' said Clare, 'they'll move on to some other story tomorrow. Try not to think about it and just get on with your life.'

Rachael looked round Clare's little study area. It was full of scraps of paper and piles of books and pamphlets. She was a proof-reader and managed to work from home, checking all these different projects for mistakes, as well as looking after Angus. It made Rachael think that it was time she found some sort of work herself, to keep her mind ticking over and to help make money for her and George.

'You're right,' she said, 'I will.'

'Oh, and there's something else I want to show you,' said Clare, 'look at this!'

She brought up a page on her computer.
'Self-defence Classes for Women', it said, with a picture in silhouette of a man attacking a woman in what appeared to be a dark alley.

'6 week beginners course, followed by an 8 week advanced course. We also offer a one day intensive course.'

Clare looked at Rachael.

'What do you reckon?' she asked, with a smile, 'it's only about twenty minutes drive from here and there's a beginners course on Wednesday mornings. We could do it while the boys are at school.'

Rachael felt a surge of excitement and empowerment. She gave Clare a hug.

'Let's do it,' she said.

Chapter Thirty-three

'Oh my God!' said the woman, peering at her phone.

'What?' asked Kate, wheeling her chair over to her mother, who was sitting on the sofa with her phone in one hand and a crisp in the other.

'It's for sale.'

'What's for sale?'

'The house where that bastard Michael Stanhope lived. Where he died. '

'Let's have a look,' said Kate taking the phone from her.

She looked at the smart house on the screen.

'Bloody Hell, look at the price!' she said, 'it can't be worth that much!'

'It can you, you know,' said her mother, 'it's in a very desirable part of London. That's what they cost these days.'

'It must be fantastic inside,' said Kate, 'I'd love to have a look. Shall we go and see round it, what do you think?'

The woman looked at her. Kate didn't know of course that her own mother was responsible for Stanhope's death. It would be madness wouldn't it to tempt fate and go and have a look round the house? Yet she suddenly felt a strong compulsion to go back there. To be in that room where she had made him pay his dues for everything he had done to Kate. To look at the floor where she had left him bleeding and see it clear of his foul presence. Removed for ever.

'Yes,' she said suddenly, 'lets do it. It'll be a bit weird, though.'

'I don't care,' said Kate, 'I want to see where he lived, especially now that he can't enjoy being there any more.'

She shook her head and handed the phone back to her mother, suddenly looking upset.

'What?' her mother asked

'It's over for him, but not for me,' she said, tightly.

'Yes, I know,' said the woman, putting her hand on Kate's shoulder.

The pain was still so raw for Kate even after all these years, she thought. She wondered how many girls he'd raped, and if they were all still suffering because of what he'd done to them. With those sort of men it was never a one-off incident. Once a rapist always a rapist. Hopefully some of his victims had been able to move on with their lives. Get married and have children. But not her Kate. She seemed stuck in a time warp. Maybe to see the house that he was no longer able to live in might help her, and she herself was already craving to look round it.

'OK,' she said, 'I'll phone the estate agent in the morning. We may have a problem with getting you up the front steps, but I'm sure we'll manage. Then you can at least see downstairs and I can take some photos of upstairs to show you later.'

The doorbell rang.

'That'll be Tony,' Kate said, her face lighting up, 'I'll get it.'

She wheeled out of the room to let him in.

The woman felt her heart sink. She hadn't known Tony was coming round. He was a nice enough guy but she had been looking forward to spending the evening with Kate. The two of them just chilling out, maybe watching television, playing scrabble. But with Tony there, she felt like a gooseberry in own house.

He seemed to be popping in more often these days. He hadn't been keen on Kate's new look on his last visit. Didn't like the false eye lashes and said he preferred her with no make-up, although he quite liked the curly hair.

He'd also been a bit rude in his reaction to the woman's changed appearance, with her short blond bob and new specs. 'I wouldn't have recognised you!' he'd said, 'what on earth have you two been up to!'

As he wheeled Kate back into the room he was at it again.

'Honestly, you look like a completely different person, now,' he said to the woman, 'have you got something to hide?'

She laughed, awkwardly.

'You should ask your Dad,' Kate said to Tony, 'he'd soon find out what it was.'

'What do you mean?' the woman asked, giving Kate a sharp look.

'Well, he's an ex-policeman!' said Kate, giving Tony's hand a squeeze, 'isn't he Tony?'

'Yeah, and a pretty good one,' said Tony proudly. 'You'll have to meet him,' he said.

The woman felt her blood run cold. An ex-policeman for fuck's sake.   This was all getting way out of hand. Too close for comfort.

'Come on in,' she said, 'nice to see you Tony.'

He's got to be dealt with, she thought, and sooner rather than later.

Chapter Thirty-four

Nana decided it was time to tackle Lorna.

'Sit down, love,' she said, after they'd cleared away the supper things. 'I want to have a little chat.'

Lorna looked at her apprehensively and perched on the arm of the sofa.

'What about?' she asked, warily.

'You were sick again this morning, weren't you? Dad and I could hear you.'

'I've told you, I've got a nasty tummy bug,' she answered defensively, her throat coming up in a bright red rash, like it always did when she was lying about something. It had been a big give-away through the years and her mother noticed it at once.

'Lorna, you don't have to pretend. You're pregnant, aren't you?'

The tears started.

'Oh, Mum, what am I going to do? Don't tell Dad will you, or Chris or Rachael?'

'Dad already knows, sweetheart. We've talked about it.'

Lorna sank down onto the sofa cushions and covered her face with her hands. She'd always been Daddy's little girl. Well, not any more. She didn't think she'd be able to face him, she felt so ashamed. It was bad enough him knowing about her affair with Michael, and now this.

'Is Chris the father or could it be Michael's?' said Nana coming straight to the point.

'I don't know, Mum, that's the problem, it could be either of them.'

More tears.

'Ssh, ssh, don't cry,' said Nana, pushing Lorna's hair back from her face. 'It's not the end of the world, we'll find a way through.'

'I can't keep it, Mum,' Lorna said, relieved to finally be able to talk about it, 'even if it was Chris's, he'd never have me back. And if it turns out to be Michael's, then what am I going to do? It would be so awful for Rachael and she's never going to forgive me anyway, especially if she finds out about the baby. Please, don't tell her. Promise.'

'Have you done a pregnancy test?' her mum asked.

'Yes, two different ones. Both positive.'

'How far gone are you?'

176

'I'm not sure. I've missed two or three periods but you know that happens with me sometimes, anyway.'

She'd always had a leaning towards an eating disorder. Fad diets and not eating for days, trying to keep herself slim. No carbs, then no fat, then no dairy. Never a settled eating routine.

'Well listen, don't do anything rash,' said Nana, 'a few more days won't make a difference. You need to think this through carefully. But whatever you decide, you know Dad and I are here to support you.'

'Thank you Mum,' said Lorna throwing her arms round her, 'you're the best.'

'Have you told anyone else about it?'

'No, nobody.'

'That's good, I'd keep it to yourself for the moment.'

'I can't have this baby, Mum,' Lorna said, desperately, 'I'm not cut out to be a single mother, I don't think I could cope. And Rachael would know it might be Michael's. It would all just be awful and Chris would be bound to find out and I'd have to go through the whole pregnancy with both of them hating me, and watching my every move. I'd have to move to Australia or something.'

'Oh don't say that, Lorna,' said Nana.

Grandad came in from the kitchen.

'Everything OK?' he asked. He looked at Nana with a silent question.

She shook her head.

'Ah,' he said, going over and giving Lorna a hug, 'don't worry, love, we'll talk it through later and decide what's for the best.'

'Sorry, I think I'm going to be sick,' said Lorna, rushing to the downstairs toilet.

§

A few seconds later, the phone rang.

'I'll get it,' said Grandad, going into the hall.

'Oh, hello Rachael, is everything alright, you sound… what?… oh I see,' his body stiffened, 'well thanks for warning us… yes, yes of course I will. You and George take care.' He put the phone down.

Nana had come through next to him, wanting to know what was going on.

He filled her in that Chris had blabbed to the press about Lorna and Michael's affair and that it was going to be all over the papers in the morning, with lurid pictures.

'Oh, my God,' said Nana sinking onto the little hard chair by the phone.

'Rachael thinks we should go away for a few days until it dies down. The press might even turn up here.'

'Well maybe we *should* go off for a bit. Stay in a hotel or something,' said Nana, worried.

'We're not going anywhere,' said Grandad firmly, 'leave the press to me.I can handle them.'

'But…' started Nana.

'We'll keep the curtains pulled and not answer the phone. They'll soon get bored,' he said. He read quite a lot of thrillers these days – he knew the form.

Lorna came out into the hall, wiping her mouth, and they told her what Chris had done. That it was all going to be in tomorrow's papers and that the press might turn up and want to talk to her.

'How can he have been such a bloody fool?' she said.

She felt sick again. This whole thing was a never-ending nightmare.

'I'm not feeling too good,' she said, retching, 'I'm going upstairs for a lie-down.'

'Alright, darling, try not to worry,' said Nana, feeling in need of a lie-down herself.

§

Next morning, there was a small group of reporters outside the front door and a note for Nana and Grandad on the kitchen table.

Dear Mum and Dad.
I've gone away for a bit. Don't worry about me, I'll be fine.
Love you loads,   Lorna xxx

Chapter Thirty-five

'Of course I can help you up the steps, no problem,' said the estate agent, looking at the attractive young lady in the wheelchair.

'Thank you,' said the woman, 'if you could take it at the bottom we could lift it together.'

'If that's alright with you, Miss,' he said to Kate politely, tucking his clip-board under his arm.

'Yes, that's fine,' she answered, smiling at him. It was nice of him to ask. He was rather good-looking; quite sexy in a funny sort of way, in his suit and tie. She bet he didn't dress like that at home. He had lovely brown eyes.

They got the chair up fairly easily. Kate felt more at ease in the chair than on crutches. She could put a rug over her lap and relax without feeling that people were looking at her missing leg.

'Light as a feather,' he said to Kate as he fished in his pocket for the keys.

'Thanks,' said Kate blushing. She'd been cutting out carbs for the last few weeks and was feeling good.

The woman winked at Kate. He seemed a nice young man. Just the sort she would have liked Kate to go out with. Instead of the dreaded Tony with his snide comments and ex-policeman father.

'We have the house to ourselves today,' the agent said, as he watched the woman manoeuvre Kate over the door step, 'the owner is not staying here at present.'

I'll bet she's not, thought the woman. Who'd want to stay in a house where your husband had been murdered.

'I'll let you show your daughter into the living room,' he said opening the door for them and putting his clipboard down on the hall table.

As they entered the room the woman felt a rush of adrenalin course through her. This was it. This is where she had stabbed him and cut his wrists. She looked down at the new elegant cream carpet. No sign of a stain, no blood seeping through. She looked at the table, remembered the sensation of being bent back over it. Remembered his contorted face, and the evil in the man. This is what her Kate had to see as he had subjected her to a life-changing horrible experience. Violent rape. She felt her breathing become rapid, the rage still simmering deep down inside her. She wondered if she was going to black-out.

'Are you alright Mum,' Kate asked, looking up at her, 'you look a bit weird.'

She passed a hand over her forehead. She was sweating.

'I'm fine thanks,' she said, pulling herself together, 'I just came over a bit dizzy.'

'I'll get you a glass of water,' said the young estate agent, making his way along the hall to the kitchen. Why these women had come to see the house was beyond him. It was obviously unsuitable for them. They needed a ground floor flat or a nice bungalow in a quiet area. Perhaps they were just drawn to seeing a house where there had been a murder and where the husband had been having an affair with the wife's sister - the lurid details had been in all the papers. Well, some people were just like that; wanted to go and gawp. Still the house was on for an exceptionally low price so someone was bound to put in an offer, before long.

'Sit down for a minute, Mum,' Kate said, 'you're probably just tired after the drive. We never had time for lunch, did we?'

She watched as her mum sat herself down on the sofa, then looked round the room. It was so strange being in the man's home. She had felt compelled to come and see it. To see where he carried on living a normal life as if nothing had happened. She wondered if there were other young girls he had raped or if it was only her. She'd probably never know. But at least she knew that he was dead. Gone forever and never coming back to find her and do it again. That had been her recurring nightmare all these years but now she could finally let it go. There was still the big mystery of who had killed him and why. There had been nothing in the papers about an arrest. Maybe they'd never find the murderer. Well, she didn't really care. He was dead now. And she was in the house where he had been killed. The reality of it suddenly made her feel sick and anxious and she wanted to leave.

'Can we go now Mum?' she asked, urgently.

'I just need to look upstairs,' said her mother, 'it'll seem odd if I don't.'

'Well I can't make the stairs,' said Kate.

'I know, but I can go up and take some photos to show you.'

'No, let's go now,' said Kate, starting to get upset.

'Here we are,' said the estate agent, bringing in a glass of water for the woman.

'Thank you,' she said.

'Shall I show you round the rest of the house?' he offered.

'No it's all right,' replied the woman. She didn't need to go upstairs anyway, she remembered the layout perfectly. She was getting worried about Kate and suddenly felt the need to quit while they were ahead, 'I think we've seen enough and I'm afraid it's not really suitable for us.'

'Oh, right,' he said, a bit wrong-footed, 'well, let me help you to your car, then.'

They suddenly heard the sound of a key in the lock and the front door opening.

'Come on, George, in we go. Home again!'

Rachael and George came straight into the living room and found the estate agent, a girl in a wheel-chair and a middle-aged woman, with a short blonde bob and glasses, all looking at them, surprised.

'Oh, I'm sorry,' said the estate agent, 'we were told at the office that you wouldn't be back until tomorrow.'

'We decided to come back today, didn't we George,' said Rachael.

She looked at George who was staring at the woman. Frozen to the spot.

It was her! Her hair was different and she was wearing glasses but it was her. The woman who'd stabbed his Daddy. He looked down at her shoes. Black with two small silver buckles.

'George?' Rachael said, 'what's the matter?'

'I'm afraid we have to leave at once,' said the woman, sensing danger, 'thank you for letting us look round.'

She swiftly wheeled Kate past them to the front door. The estate agent followed and helped her lift the wheel-chair down the steps.

'I'll be with you in a second,' he called back to Rachael.

'What a rude lady,' she said to George when they'd gone.

'She was the lady who stabbed Daddy,' said George, 'was she coming to get us?'

'Don't be silly darling, it wasn't her. She doesn't look anything like your head-mistress,' she said, ruffling his hair. She hoped this wasn't the start of him thinking every woman who came to the house was 'the lady', 'now, come on, let's get ourselves unpacked,' she said, and hurried him into the kitchen.

'She had the same shoes,' said George firmly, standing his ground, 'with the silver buckles.'

Rachael slowly turned and looked at him.

Chapter Thirty-six

'It was a stupid idea to go and look at the house,' said the woman as she drove angrily through the traffic.

The bloody child had recognised her, she was sure of it. He must have been looking through the door or something, when she'd stabbed his father. Even though she had her new blonde hair now and the glasses, she could tell by the boy's face that he knew. Something had passed between them. He was probably already telling his mother and she was more than likely, about contact the police. Shit. Shit. Shit.

'For God's sake Mum, calm down,' said Kate, 'you're going way too fast, you'll get us arrested.'

The woman came to her senses. That was the last thing she wanted.

'Sorry love,' she said, slowing down, 'I just felt it was too much for you, seeing where he lived. We'd have done better to leave well alone. It's too late now. We should just try and forget all about him.'

'Horrible, disgusting man,' said Kate, 'how could he live in that lovely house, married and with a child as well, as if nothing had happened. And how many other girls did he do it to? I wonder if his wife knew?' she went on, 'surely not or she could never have stayed with him.'

The woman had to keep reminding herself that Kate had no idea that it was she, her mother, who had killed him. Oddly she felt a sense of pride. Justice had been done. He had taken Kate's previous life away from her and now she had taken his. Fair exchange is no robbery, she told herself lifting her chin defiantly. But no amount of cream carpeting could erase the memory of his body lying in blood, coming steadily from his wrists, stomach and chest.

Now the wretched child, his mother, and the estate agent, would all be able to give a description of her new appearance to the police and before she knew it she'd be starring in 'Crime Catch Up' again. She groaned, baring her teeth.

'What?' asked Kate.

'Nothing. Just keep quiet, I'm trying to think,' she said sharply.

'OK fine, sorry I spoke,' said Kate, staring out of the window. Best not to mess when her mum got into this sort of mood.

It was time to move house again, thought the woman. Too many local people already knew her by sight, before she'd cut her hair and changed her appearance. And now people were getting to know her again, the way she looked now. One more TV showing could lead the police directly to her door. She was starting to panic, things were closing in on her.

They drove in silence for a few minutes.

'We're going to have to move again, Kate,' she said to her daughter, 'I can't keep up with the rent, I'm three months behind already.'

'On no, Mum, we can't! What about Tony?' Kate asked, horrified.

Fuck Tony, the woman thought.

'Well, he can come with us, if he wants to,' she said blithely, as she sped through a red light.

'Don't be silly Mum, we can't just up and off like that.'

'We've done it before,' said the woman.

'Yes I know but…'

'So we can do it again. We'll start packing up some stuff tonight, I'll hire a van and we'll leave at three-thirty a.m. tomorrow morning.'

'What about Tony?' Kate asked, 'he's coming round tonight to watch I'm a Celeb.'

'Text him and say you're ill,' the woman said.

'No, I want to see him,' said Kate, getting heated, 'he's my boyfriend, you can't stop me seeing him.'

'Alright then, let him come,' the woman said, thinking rapidly, 'just tell him we're going to stay with your auntie for a couple of weeks. She's broken her ankle and needs help.'

'I haven't got an auntie.'

'You have now,' said the woman hooting at the car in front who was going too slowly for her liking. Bloody white-haired useless drivers.

'I'll have to tell him where we're going,' said Kate, 'and don't let's go far, I want to keep on seeing him.'

We'll see about that, the woman thought to herself.

'Don't worry, you can text him when we get there,' she said.

Scotland, she was thinking or maybe somewhere remote in the Lake district. Maybe even right down to Cornwall. She could dye her hair red and mix in with all the arty people down there. Pretend to be an artist. Who would know. She could rustle up an abstract painting as well as anybody. She might even be able to sell a few! Make a bit of money.

She was beginning to work out a plan. She just had to sort out the Tony problem.

A solution began to form in her head. Yes. It would work.

Sorry Kate.

Goodbye Tony.

Chapter Thirty-seven

As she helped her out of the car, the woman reached into Kate's bag and slipped Kate's phone into her pocket.

The first part of the plan was underway.

When she'd got Kate into the house she made a call to a self-drive company and arranged to hire a van for two weeks. She'd collect it tomorrow at five p.m. They could pack it up after midnight, when it was dark and there weren't many people about. She'd leave her own car near the self-drive place and collect it when she returned the van.

She waited until early evening and told Kate she was nipping out to get a few things from the corner shop. She pulled the curtains and sat Kate in front of Eastenders.

'Back soon,' she said, as she slipped out of the front door.

She waited on the corner until she saw Tony approaching with a small bunch of flowers and walked up to him.

'Oh Tony, I'm so sorry,' she said, putting her hand on his arm.

'What about?' he asked, confused.

'Kate doesn't want to see you any more. She couldn't bear to tell you herself, so she's asked me to. She's met someone else.'

'I don't believe it,' he said his cheeks flushing bright red.

'I know, love, it's so upsetting but these things do happen.'

'Who is it, who has she met. Do I know him?'

'No love, it's someone from her past who's just turned up again. They were engaged for a while, didn't she tell you about him?'

'No she bloody well didn't,' he said angrily, 'well I'm going to go and see her anyway,' he said, starting to push past her.

'I wouldn't if I were you,' the woman said, holding her ground, 'he's with her now on the sofa.'

'Oh fuck,' he said, throwing the flowers into the gutter.

'There's no need to swear, love,' the woman said sharply, 'that won't solve anything. Why don't you phone her tomorrow and you can talk it through with her? She may not answer, though; she's never been very good at ending relationships.'

Tony looked at her for a moment and then turned on his heel and strode off back down the street.

The woman smiled to herself, picked up the flowers and went home.

'Oh, sweetheart, I'm so sorry,' she said to Kate as soon as she got in.

'What?' said Kate looking worried, 'what's happened?'

'It's Tony,' the woman said, 'I ran into him on the way to the shop. He asked me to give you these,' she handed Kate the flowers, which were looking a bit bedraggled after landing in the gutter.

'Why,' asked Kate, 'where is he. Isn't he coming?'

The woman came up behind Kate and gave her a long hug.

'I'm so sorry darling but he asked me tell you that he can't see you any more. He's found someone else.'

'What do you mean, he can't have!' she said, gasping and putting her hand up to her mouth.

'I know, it's really hard Kate, he must be mad, he'll never find a girl as good as you.'

'It's because of my leg isn't it?' said Kate.

'No darling, I'm sure it's not that, and if it is then he's not worth having. You're better off without him.'

'I'm going to phone him, where's my phone?' said Kate desperately looking through her bag.

'He said to tell you not to contact him,' said the woman, 'it would only make things worse.'

'Who is she, who is he seeing?' said Kate still frantically looking for her phone, 'I can't find it Mum, where's my phone?'

'Oh, God, did you leave it in town, at that coffee shop?' her Mum said, 'I think you must have, you were looking at it there. You must have left it on the table.'

'Oh no,' said Kate bursting into tears, 'I can't believe this is happening.'

'It's alright sweetheart,' said the woman, rubbing her shoulders, 'there'll be other boyfriends, much better than him. And hopefully your phone will turn up soon.'

'What am I going to do,' said Kate, covering her face with her hands.

'Start packing,' said the woman firmly, 'come on it'll take your mind off him. It'll be fun. We're off on another of our adventures!'

She gave Kate a kiss on the top of her head and went into the kitchen to make a cup of tea. While the kettle boiled, she took Kate's phone out of her pocket, put it into an empty fish cakes packet and dropped it into the bottom of the rubbish bin.

Chapter Thirty-eight

Rachael phoned the police. She told them George was insisting that the lady who'd come to look at the house was the same one who'd stabbed his father.

They were particularly interested by the fact that she had been accompanied by a young woman in a wheelchair. There could be a connection to a couple that had been observed at the other side of the graveyard, during the funeral. A woman in a headscarf pushing a girl in a wheelchair.

They sent the fingerprint team back to the house to see if there were fresh prints that might match up. There were, and they did.

It was her. Michael Stanhope's killer.

They interviewed the young estate agent. It turned out that the details the woman had given him were false. However, after he'd helped get the wheelchair down the steps of the house, he had watched them go to their car and, on instinct, had taken a photo of them and the number plate, while they were busy folding up the chair to put it in the boot. There had been something strange about their sudden departure when the owner came back unexpectedly. He'd wondered if there was some burglary scam going on or something. He'd then forgotten all about it when he went on to his next viewing.

However, he was able to give the police the registration number.

This had now been checked and an alert had gone out among the force to look out for the car and report it immediately if it was found.

Three days later, it was spotted near a self-drive firm. They checked with the owner and showed him the photo of the woman. The guy on the desk confirmed it was her and that she'd taken a transit van for two weeks, and she'd paid in advance by cash. The personal details she had given turned out to be false.

Now the police had the number of the van and an alert went round to report back if it was seen anywhere. Of course, it could be some distance away by now.

They had an unmarked police car parked 24/7 in the road where the woman's car had been left, in case she came back to collect it. Although they reckoned the likelihood was that she'd just abandon it and then later abandon the van. But you never know. This woman was a murderer. She had to be caught and soon, before she killed anyone else. She had also attempted to kill the doctor's son and left him for dead. Had he not survived she would be up for a double murder.

They were also concerned about the boy, George. If the woman had realised that he recognised her, then he might be in danger. She might decide that he needed to be silenced rather than be free to give evidence against her. It would be the thought of a warped and dangerous mind but then that was what they were dealing with.

They advised Rachael to take George back to stay with Clare and Angus for the time being, if possible. Just until they had caught the woman. It shouldn't be too long now, they informed her; they were closing the net. It would be hard for the woman to go unnoticed for long, since she had the girl in the wheelchair with her, who they thought could be her daughter.

They got a new E-FIT done of the woman with her changed appearance and also one of her daughter, with the help of Rachael and the estate agent, and told them that they were going to show them on the evening news that night, along with a description of the hire van.

The heat was on.

§

That night, Tony was sitting on the sofa with his dad, looking at his phone while his father watched the news. He lifted his eyes to the TV for a minute and saw the E-FIT of the woman filling the screen.

'That's Kate's mum!' he said in shock.

'I hope you're wrong son, she's a murderess,' said his dad, 'stabbed a man to death.'

'It *is* her and oh God, that's Kate!' Tony said, as they brought up a side view of the two of them, by the woman's car.

They both watched, leaning forward and taking in every word, learning that Kate and her mother were now on the run. The programme then moved on to the weather.

They sat for a moment in stunned silence.

'Are you absolutely sure, Tony?' his dad said, turning off the television.

'Yes, definitely. It's them.'

'Right,' said his dad, 'this is important. We need to move quickly.'

He strode over to the land-line and picked up the phone. His years with the police, coming into play.

'I know exactly who to phone. They'll put me straight through,' he said.

'That's why she said Kate wouldn't see me,' said Tony, his mind racing over what they'd just said on the TV, 'I don't think there was any fiancée, she was just trying to take Kate away with her.'

'Just a minute, son, just wait till I've got through to the right department.'

'Dad,' said Tony, frantically, 'what if she murders Kate?'

Chapter Thirty-nine

Rachael checked that it was OK with Clare, then they grabbed a few things and went straight over to her. It was chilling to think that the woman who had killed Michael had actually been there in her home, and talked to her face to face. The police were certain it was the woman they were looking for and they didn't want to take any chances in case she targeted George. She might have realised he'd recognised her. She was obviously unhinged and there was no way of knowing what she might do next.

Against their advice, Rachael went back to the house the next morning, while George was still at school, to pick up some more clothes and toys. She felt quite jumpy and looked carefully up and down the street before she got out of the car. She let herself in, turned off the alarm and went upstairs to find the things they needed, when the doorbell rang.

She nearly jumped out of skin. Who the hell was it? Was it the woman? She felt sick. She took some deep breaths. After a moment she went slowly and quietly down the stairs, crept along the hall and looked through the peep-hole.

It was Duncan! She couldn't believe it; after all these years. She opened the door, hugged him hard and held on tight for several moments.

'Hey, there!' he said, 'you can't have missed me that much!'

'Oh, I'm so sorry. I thought you might be someone else and I was really scared,' she said, laughing and feeling a bit embarrassed, 'come on in.'

Duncan was a really lovely man. They'd been together for two years at college and then he'd gone to university up in Newcastle, and they stupidly decided to break up, so they could both feel free while they were apart. She remembered thinking at the time that maybe it was for the best, that perhaps he was just too nice for her. She was looking for someone more exciting with a hint of danger. Then she'd met Michael and all her troubles started. Be careful what you wish for!

She made them both a cup of tea and they sat on the sofa together. She remembered the smell of his jacket. Still the same one.

She filled him in on everything that had happened.

'I've only just caught up with it all,' he said, 'I've been away in South Africa for six months. When I came back I saw the story on the news and realised to my horror that it was you. I still had your Mum and Dad's number, so I phoned them and said I wanted to contact you and they gave me your address, 'I'm so sorry,' he said, looking earnestly in her eyes, 'what a terrible, horrible time for you.'

Her eyes filled with tears.

'Come here,' he said and enfolded her in his arms.

It felt so natural to be with him. After a few minutes, he brushed her hair back from her face and kissed her gently.

She found herself responding to him in the same old familiar way.

'I've never stopped thinking about you,' he said.

She told him about her marriage to Michael and how unhappy he had made her. How he had become violent towards her and that she'd wanted to leave him but had been too frightened.

'You poor thing,' said Duncan, stroking her face.

They talked non-stop for about two hours losing all track of time and it was as if they'd never been apart.

'Do you want to see upstairs?' she said eventually.

He looked at her.

'Are you sure?' he asked, 'it's not too soon for you?'

'I'm sure,' said Rachael, smiling at him.

The love-making was wonderful. As it always had been when they were together. Urgent and thrilling but still caring and loving. So unlike Michael and his forceful dominance.

For the first time in years she felt happy.

Two hours later she woke up sleepily, and turned her head to see a dark haired man half turned away from her.

'Oh, my God,' she thought, 'he's still alive,' she felt sick for a moment until she realised that it wasn't Michael, it was Duncan. Her Duncan; her old boyfriend!

Slowly her thoughts came together and she realised that it was the middle of the afternoon, and the weak sun was showing through the closed shutters.

'Hi beautiful,' he said as he woke up, 'God I've I missed you.'

He turned over and gave a series of gentle kisses all over her face.

'Duncan, wait a minute,' she said laughing and holding him away from her, 'what time is it? I'm supposed to be collecting George and Angus from school at four thirty.'

'Well, you've got fifteen minutes to get there,' he said looking at his watch, 'do you want me to drive you?'

'No, hang on,' she said, reaching for her phone in the pocket of her jeans, which were in a pile on the floor. She rang Clare and asked if she could possibly collect the boys for her, even though she knew it was her turn.'

'Yes, of course I can,' said Clare, 'what's up?'

'Something fantastic. I'll tell you as soon as I get back to yours.'

'You sound a bit breathless and strange,' said Clare, 'are you alright?'

'More than alright,' said Rachael, smiling at Duncan.

'Wow! can't wait to hear!' said Clare, 'Look, I'd better go and get the boys. Don't feel you have to rush back. I'll take them to footie training after tea. Come back when you're ready. Bye. Don't do anything rash!' she added as an afterthought.

Too late, thought Rachael. I already have.

She put the phone on the bedside table and turned back to Duncan.

Chapter Forty

The Woman had driven them through the night down the M4 and on towards Wiltshire. Kate had slept for most of the way, exhausted by the whole packing process and the emotional distress of Tony having apparently dumped her. She still couldn't believe it and was desperate to find her phone so she could contact him and find out what had happened.

As it started to get light, the Woman made her way to a remote farmhouse that offered bed and breakfast. She remembered it from years ago when she had been looking for somewhere to hide in the area. It would be perfect to stay for a few days and keep the transit van out of sight in case the police were looking for her. It would also give her a chance to work out her next move. Hopefully to find somewhere equally remote that she could rent for a year and then just lie low. She would keep Kate indoors, maybe having to partially sedate her, and go out by herself when she needed to, having changed her appearance yet again.

The B&B was run by a couple of eccentric sisters who only had two single rooms which they occasionally let out to walkers. One was on the ground floor which would be good for Kate and the other was upstairs, which would work for her. Most importantly they didn't have a television. No time for it, they'd told her.

The sisters were already up, feeding the pigs, when they arrived. Their hair was sticking up all over the place and their clothes were a mixture of old fashioned tank tops, baggy trousers and shirts, all a bit mucky. They both had Wellington boots with massive thick socks rolling over the top.

They were delighted to see them.

'We don't have much company these days,' said Maisie, the eldest sister, 'come on in, we'll make you some bacon and eggs for breakfast….mind the chickens,' she said as they helped Kate out of the van and into her wheelchair.

'You can stay as long as you like,' said Sandie, the younger of the two, 'we've no bookings at the moment. Nobody wants to walk at this time of the year… sorry,' she said to Kate in her wheelchair, 'bloody stupid thing to say.'

Kate smiled.

'It's OK,' she said, 'I'm fine about it, really.'

'Good girl,' said Sandie, 'that's the spirit.'

They went indoors and had a large breakfast, then the Woman went upstairs to have a lie-down. She was knackered after the packing and the driving. She left Kate to have a rest in the downstairs bedroom and said she'd take her for a walk in her chair later on that morning.

The moment her mother had gone upstairs, Kate lay wide awake, trying to work out what the hell was going on. Her mother seemed to have lost it. She was behaving so strangely and wouldn't tell her where they were going or what their future plans were. She desperately missed Tony and couldn't bear being without her phone. She'd asked her mother if she could use hers but she said the battery was flat and that she'd lost her charger. Until now, Kate hadn't realised how addicted she was **to her phone.** Without it, she felt cut off from the world.

Maisie popped her head round the door.

'You alright?' she asked, 'anything you need?'

Kate thought quickly. This was her chance.

'Well, I wonder if I could possibly make a quick call from your phone?' she asked, 'I'm happy to pay for it.'

She'd noticed the land-line on the hall table as they came in.

'Of course you can,' said Maisie, feeling sorry for the poor girl, 'you don't have to pay, you can have it on us. Unless it's a call to Australia!'

Kate laughed, 'no, only to London,' she said, 'I'll keep it short.'

'Hang on, I'll bring it in. It's hands free you know,' she said proudly, 'we got it earlier this year. Some chap came to stay for a couple of weeks and got it in for us. I take it with me when I'm feeding the chickens. Brilliant isn't it, modern technology?'

'Brilliant!' Kate echoed as Maisie went into the hall and came back with the phone.

'I'll leave you to it,' said Maisie, handing it to her, 'Sandie and I are about to nip out for a bit to get some provisions, so just leave it on the bedside table when you've finished.'

'Thank you so much,' said Kate as Sandie went out, closing the door behind her.

Kate knew Tony's phone number off by heart, and she dialled straight away.

'Hello,' came Tony's voice.

Her heart missed a beat. If he'd really wanted to end it, he might not want to talk to her.

'Hi, Tony, it's me,' she said in a tremulous voice.

'Oh, my God, Kate, are you alright? I've been so worried about you, where are you?'

'I'm in Wiltshire, I think. Tony, did you really want to finish with me?' she asked, straight out.

'God no, Kate. Your Mum said you wanted to end it and that you were seeing someone else.'

Kate was stunned. How could her mother have done that to her.

'That's so not true,' said Kate, 'Mum said you didn't want to see me any more. I'm so sorry.'

'I love you Kate.'

'I love you too,' said Kate, her eyes filling up.

'Listen Kate, your Mum's in big trouble. She's wanted by the police.'

'What do you mean? What for?'

'She's wanted for the murder of a man in London and also a possible attempted murder of a young guy in Guildford.'

Kate felt as if she was about to pass out. Suddenly everything became clear. This was it. This explained her Mum changing her appearance, the obsession with going to London to look round the house. The need for the sudden move. Her Mum had killed Michael, the man who had raped her. She had killed him. Oh, God, she had killed him. And who was this other man in South London. What did he have to do with it?

'I don't know what to do,' said Kate, shaking.

'Just stay put, if you can,' said Tony, 'Dad and I are going to come and pick you up. We'll look after you until this is all sorted out, OK?'

'Thank you,' said Kate, 'look I'm going to have to go, I can hear Mum coming down the stairs.'

'Where are you?' Tony asked urgently.

Kate saw a card on the bedside table.

'The Chicken Coop, B&B,' she said.

'Post code?'

She read it out it to him and then turned off the phone and hid it under her pillow.

'Hello Kate,' said the Woman, opening the door and coming in to the room, holding a big puffy pillow, 'everything OK?'

'Yes it's fine,' said Kate, looking at her Mum and thinking; she killed him. And did she kill someone else as well? Was she now planning to kill her? Her mother had always looked after her and cared for her but she'd been acting so strangely, lately. Was she actually a psychopath or something? She suddenly felt really frightened.

'I thought you might need this,' said her mother approaching the bed with the pillow.

Chapter Forty-one

Rachael was sitting at the kitchen table, finishing an early supper with Clare and the two boys, when her phone rang.

'Sorry guys, I'd better get this, it might be the estate agent,' she said going to get her mobile off the coffee table.

She'd finally had an offer on the house and it looked promising. A cash buyer who wanted to complete in eight weeks.

She picked up her phone and looked at the screen.

'Oh my God, it's Lorna,' she said taking it into the hall.

'Lorna, where are you, are you OK?' she asked

She and her parents hadn't heard from her since she'd walked out at five months pregnant, telling them all not to worry about her. They'd been frantic, of course. Not knowing where she was or even if she was still in the country. She'd taken her passport with her when she left, so they thought she may have gone abroad. Their mum had taken it very hard.

'I lost the baby,' Lorna said flatly.

'Oh, Lorna, I'm so sorry,' said Kate, 'are you alright, where have you been?'

'In Holland,' she said.

'Well, where are you now, can we meet up?'

'I wondered if I could come and stay with you for a bit,' Lorna said, in a very subdued voice, 'I can't face going back to Mum and Dad at the moment.'

'Oh God, well - um - it's a bit complicated right now. I'm not living at home. George and I are staying with my friend Clare.'

'Why? What's happened?'

'It's to do with the woman who killed Michael. She turned up at the house and the police have told us to move out until they've caught her.'

'Oh shit,' said Lorna.

'Yes, I know. Look, tell me where you are and we can meet and sort something out.'

'Don't bother, I'm fine thanks,' said Lorna, shortly, and cut off the call.

'Damn,' said Rachael going back into the kitchen.

'Trouble?' asked Clare, turning the TV on for the boys.

Rachael filled her in as they cleared the table and **loaded** the dishwasher.

'She could always come here for a bit,' said Rachael, 'she can sleep on the sofa. Ring her back.'

'She won't answer,' said Rachael.

'Try,' said Clare.

Rachael pretended to dial the number.

'No reply,' she said, turning her phone off and putting it back on the coffee table.

Firstly, she couldn't put that extra strain on Clare, but also she knew she couldn't bear to be living in the same house as Lorna. She got a flash of Lorna in bed with Michael tangled up in the lilac silk sheets. She tried to shut it out of her mind.

'I've got to give Mum and Dad a ring,' she said, 'they've been so worried about her, especially Mum.'

'Yes, of course,' said Clare, 'use the land line, you'll get a better reception.'

'Thanks.' said Rachael going back into the hall and shutting the door behind her.

She sat on the stairs for a minute, trying to work out her how she felt about Lorna losing the baby. Possibly Michael's baby. Her first feeling, when Lorna told her, had been a sense of relief. How awful to feel that, about her own sister losing her baby. But it would have been hard to watch the child growing up, maybe looking the spitting image of Michael. Having to pretend to George that Aunty Lorna's baby was his cousin instead of a half brother or sister.

She shook her head, appalled at herself, and dialled the number for her parents. They would be relieved to know Lorna was safe, but now they were going to have to deal with the loss of their second grandchild. She felt sad for them. They didn't need all this trouble. She was also sorry for Lorna. Despite everything she'd done, she didn't deserve this.

After the call she came back into the kitchen and Clare handed her a glass of wine.

'Did they take it OK' she asked.

'Well, they were upset about the baby of course but relieved that Lorna was safe. Mum even said maybe it's for the best. I know she's been worrying so much about how it was all going to turn out.'

'OK, let's take your mind off it for a bit. Tell me what's been going on.'

'What do you mean?' said Rachael, aware the colour was rising in her cheeks.

'Come on, tell me about Duncan!'

Chapter Forty-two

The Woman approached Kate's bed holding the pillow out.

'You might want an extra one,' she said, smiling, her head on one side.

Kate shook her head, 'I'm fine thanks,' she answered uneasily.

'Come on, sit up a bit,' said her mother, leaning over her.

As she did so the phone that Kate had borrowed, fell to the floor.

The woman looked at it and then back at Kate.

'And who does this belong to, might I ask?' she said, picking it up and holding it towards Kate.

'I borrowed it from Maisie,' said Kate looking at her, nervously.

'Don't tell me you've been phoning Tony. Have you, you stupid girl?' the Woman asked, raising her voice and going red in the face.

'I'm sorry, I just really wanted to speak to him,' said Kate shrinking back away from her.

'I told you, he doesn't want anything to do with you,' her mother said, slamming the pillow down hard on the end of the bed, 'don't you believe anything I tell you?' she went on, shaking Kate by the arm, 'don't you ever listen to me. Did you get through to him, what did he say?'

'There was no reply,' said Kate thinking quickly.

She didn't know what the hell was going on or what might happen next but all she could do was try and keep her mother calm until Tony and his Dad arrived. Hopefully the police too. Should she warn her mother? No, she decided, her mum might freak out.

'Sorry Mum,' she said, 'I wont try and phone him again, I promise.'

'When I think of all the things I do for you, and this is the way you repay me,' said the Woman, noticing that a small card had slipped to the floor. She picked it up and saw that it was the B&B's card with the address on it.

She took a long look at Kate. She didn't believe her. Kate had lied to her, she had spoken to Tony and probably told him where they were staying. If Tony had seen the television coverage, he might even call the police and tell them where she and Kate were hiding out. This was going to ruin everything. Stupid, stupid girl. She was becoming a liability.

She made a snap decision

'Come on,' she said briskly, 'we're going for a walk, we need some fresh air.'

'I don't want go for a walk,' Kate said.

'Yes, you do,' said the Woman, bringing the wheelchair to the side of the bed. She got hold of Kate, roughly, and hoiked her into it, then fixed the strap across her.

Kate was protesting but her mother completely ignored her and wheeled her out into the hall, then bumped the chair down the front steps and onto the path. She had to get them away as soon as possible. If the police had been informed by Tony of where they were staying, they could turn up at any minute.

She'd seen Maisie and Sandie driving off in a car, from the upstairs window, and noticed that there was a mud splattered old Ford van parked outside as well. She went quickly back into the hall and looked for any sort of key holder. Success. There were a couple of keys on it, one with a tag that said 'the van'.

She ran upstairs and grabbed her handbag, then rushed down into the front garden.

'Mum, what are you doing. What's going on? Take me back indoors. I don't want to go out.' Kate shouted at her.

The Woman ignored her and tried the keys. The driver's door opened easily.

She wheeled Kate to the passenger side and lifted her, bodily, into the front seat.

'No, no, I don't want to go!' she screamed.

'Oh, shut up Kate,' she said and gave her a hard slap across the face, 'this is all your fault anyway,' she went on, 'we would have been safe here, but now we've got to leave everything and go on the bloody run again.'

She slammed the door shut.

Kate was now terrified. She knew Tony and his Dad couldn't arrive for at least a couple of hours. Maybe if they'd told the police, a local station would send someone, that was her only hope.

'Please let me out, Mum,' she begged, holding her cheek, 'you go if you want to, but leave me here. I'm only a nuisance anyway.'

'No way,' said the Woman, getting into the car, 'you know too much.'

She started the engine and they roared off down the long narrow leafy track leaving Kate's wheelchair behind, fallen over on it's side. Once away from the B&B and on the roads, any police cars they passed would be looking for the self-hire transit not a small, dirty, navy van. Good work, she complimented herself, smiling.

She's gone mad, thought Kate. She needs to be taken into a psychiatric hospital or something. If we stop for any reason, for petrol or whatever, I'm going start screaming until someone comes to see what the matter is. I'll tell them to call the police, and that she's kidnapped me. She realised that her hands were shaking.

The Woman could hear a police siren in the distance and felt the adrenalin pumping through her. She drove at speed along the lanes, going deeper and deeper into the countryside. She opened her window and let the wind come rushing into the car. She could hear a helicopter overhead and she started laughing, going faster and faster.

Chapter Forty-three

The crash, when it came, was horrific.

The woman was going too fast round a corner. She skidded off the road, crossed over the bank, and drove head-first into a large tree.

The impact crushed the bonnet of the van and The Woman shot forward through the window as it smashed against the trunk. In her haste to get away, she hadn't worn her seat belt. She had felt invincible, laughing, sure that nothing and no-one could catch her.

Kate had managed to put her belt on as soon as she realised that her mother was driving recklessly. After the crash, she sat in shocked silence for a moment.

'Mum?' she finally whispered, looking in horror at her mother, who had ricocheted back into her seat, her face caved in, unrecognisable, blood pouring down over her chest and onto her lap. Her head had lolled over to the passenger side and Kate could see that her eyes were glazed. Her body looked twisted against the driver's door and she was completely still. There was no sign of breathing. Kate knew at once, she was dead.

She herself was covered in broken glass, bits of snapped branches, and splashes of blood from her mother. She made herself look down at her good leg to see if it was all mangled up but there was no pain and it looked OK. It seemed that she was alright although her neck was hurting. The driver's side had taken the impact of the crash.

She tried to get her senses together. What should she do? Was the van about to burst into flames. 'Oh God, please help me,' she said.

She was able to undo her seat belt, and managed to open the door and lift her leg out, hanging on the door for balance but then fell heavily onto the ground as she tried to get out. She landed painfully on her left shoulder, then rolled onto her front and using her elbows and forearms managed to drag herself away from the van and towards the road. If only she had her crutches she thought, she was so bloody helpless without them. She prayed that someone driving by would stop, and help, and get her mother out of the car.

She lay there, collapsed, with her head on the grassy verge and was aware of a massive silence apart from a few birds singing. It was as if the world had stopped. After a while it started to rain and it was strangely comforting and soothing. She felt as if she was slipping into a helpless state of peace.

Suddenly there was the sound of urgent police sirens. She tried to call out, but of course they wouldn't be able to hear her. There was nothing she could do but wait. They were coming nearer. She was aware that the helicopter was whirring above her again. Of course they were looking for a murderer. Her mother! It didn't seem possible. It was like some terrible nightmare and she'd wake up back in their old home. Before the rape, before she'd ever met Michael, before she'd lost her leg.

Two police cars approached from one direction and another from the opposite side. They all screamed to a halt as they got near and police men and women got out of their cars and ran towards her.

'My mother is still in the van!' she said desperately, 'I couldn't get her out.'

'Don't worry love, leave it us,' one of the men said, 'we'll do everything we can.'

Then a policewoman came and put a silver blanket over her and held her hand.

'What's your name, sweetheart?' she asked.

'Kate,' she answered, starting to shake uncontrollably.

'It's Kate,' the policewoman said to one of the men nearby. He immediately spoke into his handset, 'Yes it's Kate. Confirmed,' he said.

'Don't worry love, the ambulance is on it's way.'

'No, no, I'm fine,' said Kate, 'it's my mother, I think she's dead.'

She started sobbing and the policewoman put an arm round her.

'It's best to get you checked out at the hospital, anyway, love,' she said, starting to stand up.

'Don't leave me,' said Kate, hanging on to her hand, 'I can't walk, I lost my leg and I don't have my crutches.'

Suddenly there was a massive explosion and the van burst into flames.

'BACK, BACK everyone', someone shouted.

'Mum!' screamed Kate.

'It's alright love, they've got her out,' said the policewoman, looking across to where they had the Woman laid out on the grass on the other side of the road. One of the men looked across at her and shook his head, then gave her a thumbs down gesture. They hadn't been able to save her.

'She'd dead, isn't she?' said Kate, 'I could tell.'

'Come on sweetheart, hang on in there, the ambulance is here.'

Within seconds, the crew had got out and come rushing over to Kate.

'She's called Kate, she's in shock and she's an amputee,' the policewoman told them.

'Got it,' said the guy, bending down next to her.

'OK Kate, we'll look after you,' he said, 'you're in safe hands.'

As she was lifted carefully into the ambulance, Kate craned her head to try and catch a last glimpse of her mother.

She couldn't see her. Only a dark green tarpaulin lying over where her body had been.

She was gone.

Chapter Forty-four

'We have some information concerning your husband's killer,' the Chief Inspector told Rachael over the phone.

'Oh my God, have you found her?' said Rachael, her pulse quickening.

'Well...' he hesitated, 'if you would like to come to the station at your earliest convenience we can fill you in on all the details, I think that would be the best plan.'

'Yes, alright,' said Rachael, uncertainly, 'could I come now, this morning?'

'That would be fine, shall we say eleven o'clock?' he asked.

'Yes, I'll be there,' she said, and hung up.

She wondered why he couldn't tell her over the phone. It must be something important for him to call her in to the station. She'd already dropped George at school, so she told Clare that there seemed to be some big news about the Woman and that she was going in to see the Chief Inspector.

'How intriguing,' said Clare, 'well don't worry about the boys, I'll pick them up from school, take as long as you need.'

'Thanks,' said Rachael.

§

When the Chief Inspector brought her up to date with the news about the crash, and the fact that the Woman was dead, Rachael felt suddenly dizzy and thought she might pass out.

'Are you alright?' he asked, 'you've gone a little pale.'

'I'm fine,' she said, taking a deep breath, 'are you sure it was her,' she asked, 'the woman who killed Michael?'

'Quite sure,' he said, 'we've already checked her fingerprints and they match those we found at the scene of the murder. Also her daughter, the girl in the wheelchair who visited your house, was in the van with her when it crashed.'

'Oh my God, did she survive?' asked Rachael.

'Fortunately, yes,' he answered, 'she's currently in hospital suffering from shock and an injured shoulder, plus various cuts and bruises. There's also a possibility of an internal injury. We will be interviewing her again shortly. She claims she had no knowledge of her mother's crime and had no part in it.'

'Then how will we ever find out why her mother killed him?' Rachael asked.

'We may never know the answer to that question,' he said, 'but the important thing is, that the woman is no further threat to you or your child. You are free to return to your house and I hope you will be able to feel safe there from now on.'

He stood, obviously anxious to return to other duties and Rachael rose with him.

She had so many unanswered questions swimming around in her head but realised that now was not the time to discuss them with him.

'However, the case is far from closed,' he said, 'and rest assured that we will be in touch if we have any further information coming from the daughter, or from my team. Until then, I wish you and your son well.'

He went to the door of the interview room and ushered her out.

§

Bloody hell, thought Rachael as she drove back to Clare's. So that's it then. Game over. She couldn't believe that after the drama of tracking the woman down over the last few months, it had all ended so suddenly. Of course, now she could never be brought to justice. And where did it leave the poor daughter? Was it true that she knew nothing about her mother's intentions? Well she'd just have to leave it to the police. She wondered how interested they would actually be in pursuing the case, now that the woman was dead.

Well, at least she and George could move back home now without feeling scared. Clare had been a fantastic support but she was desperate to get back to her own space and find some sort of normality again. George and Angus would miss being together, but they could always go to each other's houses after school.

The next thing on the list was to introduce George to Duncan!

Chapter Forty-five

together, but they could always go to each other's houses after
school.

The next thing on the list was to introduce George to Duncan!

All through the first night in the hospital, Kate kept waking up
and trying decide what to tell the police. Her shoulder was
agony and the painkillers didn't seem to be strong enough to
last until the next lot were brought round. The police had told
her they would be in to talk to her in the morning and she felt
scared. Would they think she was an accomplice in Michael
Stanhope's murder?

She decided to tell them the truth about everything. About
being raped when she was seventeen, and how she'd seen the
man who did it on television and recognised him. How her
Mum had gone ballistic and swore she'd find him and make
him pay for what he'd done. She told them that her mother had
gone to London with the intention of blackmailing him but had
arrived too late. Someone had murdered him.

She'd tell them that she and her Mum had gone to the funeral
and they'd watched from a distance as he was lowered into the
ground. And what a huge sense of relief she'd felt knowing
that he could never turn up and do it to her again.

Then she'd explain how she and her Mum had discovered that
the house he'd lived in was for sale and how they'd both felt
the need to go and see what kind of life he'd been enjoying;
having destroyed hers and leaving her so traumatised that
she'd jumped out of a window and had to have her leg

amputated as a result, because she was so frightened that another man might do the same thing to her.

All these memories were drifting in and out of her mind as she felt the drugs have an effect and then wane. When it was finally morning, after what felt to have been the longest night of her life, she stuck her arm out for the latest blood pressure check from the nurse and felt she was ready to face the police.

'You'll be able to go home in a few days,' said the nurse, jotting down the reading.

'I can't go home,' she said, thinking of the midnight flit in the transit van. She realised she had no home to go to.

'Oh come on, you'll be fine,' said the nurse, with a distinct lack of interest, 'I'm off duty now, so I'll see you tomorrow night,' she said, bustling out of the room.

When the police arrived to interview her, she sat up as best she could, answered all their questions about the crash and the recent events leading up to it, then told them the whole story, starting with the rape.

The Chief Inspector listened intently all the way through without interrupting her, making occasional notes. They were also recording the whole thing.

When she'd finished there was a long pause.

'Tell me again what year it was, that this rape happened?' he asked.

She told him.

'Are you quite sure that was the year?'

'Yes,' she said, 'I was seventeen, in the sixth form.'

The Chief Inspector got up from his chair and walked to the window. He entered something in his phone. After a few moments he turned round to face her.

'I'm afraid I'm having some difficulty in believing your story, young lady,' he said.

'What do you mean?' said Kate in confusion. What was this? She'd told him the truth, why wouldn't he believe her?

'During the year that you mention,' he said gravely, 'Michael Stanhope, the man that your mother murdered and who you accuse of having raped you, was living and working in Canada. He made no trips to England during that time.

Kate put her hand to her mouth in shock and horror. She had been so sure it was him. He'd looked the same, sounded the same. Now the police would think she was involved in his murder.

And worse than that.

Her mother had murdered the wrong person and the man who raped her was still out there.

Chapter Forty-six

The child was feeling cross.

He could hear Mummy talking and laughing downstairs with the new man. Duncan, he was called.

He was glad that Mummy was happy, but she should be laughing and having fun with him, not the man. It made him angry. He punched his pillow.

After all this time he was finally back in his own bedroom with his toys but now he felt lonely without Angus for company. It had been fun, them sharing a room in Clare's house. He liked Clare. She was kind and funny and Mummy liked her too. So why did they have to leave and come back to this old house where his Daddy had been killed by that horrid lady. Mummy said that the lady was never coming back because she'd died in a car crash.

If the lady and Daddy were both dead, would they have to meet each other in Heaven? Would Daddy be scared that she would hurt him again? Had Mummy been scared when Daddy used to hurt *her*? He had been scared of Daddy. When he got cross, he had this really angry face, it wasn't nice to be near him. He used to hide from him in the cupboard under the stairs, but sometimes Daddy found him and pulled him out and hit him on the back of his legs. It hurt. It made him cry.

When he and Mummy had come back from Clare's last night, it had been really fun. Mummy cooked some macaroni cheese which was his favourite. And they had watched TV snuggled up on the sofa, under a rug, like they used to.

But today, as they drove home from school, Mummy said this friend called Duncan was coming to tea and that George would really like him.

He didn't.

He didn't want anyone else in the house. Just him and Mummy. And when Duncan had arrived and they all sat in the kitchen having tea, Mummy had not been like she usually was. She had been all giggly and sharing jokes with Duncan. And she kept flicking her hair back in a funny way and her cheeks got pink.

George didn't understand what was going on.

Then Mummy had put him to bed earlier than usual and now he could smell something delicious wafting up from the kitchen. Maybe shepherd's pie, which he really liked.

So Duncan was staying for supper.

He heard Mummy coming upstairs and she popped her head round the door.

'Are you alright, sweetheart,' she said, 'are you still awake?'

'Is Duncan staying for supper?' he asked.

'Yes he is. He's nice isn't he, did you like him?'

'He's not staying the night is he?' said George, sulkily.

'No darling, not tonight,' his mother said, coming over and tucking him in, where he'd kicked off his covers. She headed back to the open door.

'Mummy,' George said, whispering urgently.

'What is it darling?' she said, giving a small sigh.

'I don't want another Daddy.'

Chapter Forty-seven

A couple of days later, Rachael dropped George off at school after a rather tricky ride with him.

Duncan had stayed the night. It wasn't the plan, but they'd had a great evening going back over old times, and ended up making love, whispering like naughty schoolchildren, so as not to wake George. They agreed that Duncan would leave soon afterwards, so as not to upset George in the morning.

It was fantastic sex, mind blowing, and afterwards they fell into a deep sleep only to be woken by George bursting into the room at six o'clock.

'Come on Mummy, get up. It's 'show and tell' today and we've got to try and finish my rocket.'

He screeched to a halt when he realised that Duncan was lying in the bed next to Mummy. He saw that he didn't have pyjamas on and Mummy wasn't wearing her nightie.

'No,' he said to Duncan, frowning, 'you shouldn't be here. Go away.'

He started pulling at the duvet.

'Don't be silly George,' said Rachael, leaping out of bed and grabbing her dressing gown off the back of the door, 'come here and give me hug,' she knelt down and pulled him into her arms.

'It's alright darling. Duncan's my friend, he's a nice man and you know what? He might be able to help you put the last bit of the rocket together. He's very clever like that.'

George looked dubiously at Duncan.

'Are you?' he asked.

'Sure thing,' said Duncan. He managed to grab his boxers and slip them on under the covers, then leapt out of bed, 'I'm ace with rockets,' he said with a big smile.

'Tell you what,' he went on, 'lets have a race and see who can get dressed first.'

'OK,' said George, after a moment's hesitation, 'I bet I win,' he shouted, racing off to his room.

'Well done,' said Rachael, to Duncan.

She was mortified by what had happened. It was last thing she wanted, for George to find them in bed together.

'Do you think it's going to scar him for life,' she said, pulling on some pants, a T-shirt and jeans.

'I'm sure he'll be fine,' said Duncan, hurriedly getting into his trousers, 'kids are more resilient than we think.'

'I win!' shouted George as he ran back into the room all dressed apart from his socks.

'Well done,' said Duncan, 'come on let's go downstairs and sort out that rocket.'

He went straight down into the kitchen with George racing behind him and Rachael following, feeling relieved that the crisis had been averted. At least for the moment.

Duncan managed to bind the top of the rocket, where the glue hadn't stuck properly, with some gaffer tape, then he and George drew a bold pattern over it with a red permanent marker they found in the pen pot, so it looked as if it was meant to be like that.

'It looks really good,' said George, beaming with pride.

'Yeah, you've done a great job with it mate,' said Duncan, smiling at Rachael.

§

In the car on the way to school, George sat in the front passenger seat, holding the rocket carefully on his lap.

'Why were you and Duncan all bare?' he said after a few moments.

'Well,' said Rachael, taking a moment to think of an answer, 'it was really hot, last night, I think there must be something wrong with the radiator in my room. I'll get it sorted out today.'

It certainly had been hot, she thought to herself with a small smile. No lie there.

'My room was alright,' said George.

'Good,' said Rachael.

George looked down at the rocket. He was very pleased with it.

'Will Duncan be there when I get home from school,' he asked after a bit.

Rachael's heart sank. Was this going to develop into a big problem?

'He might be,' she said lightly as they turned a corner.

'Do you think he likes Lego?'

'I'm sure he does,' said Rachael, breathing a sigh of relief, 'you could build something together.'

'Yes,' said George, 'oh, look, there's Angus, can we stop?'

'Hang on,' said Rachael, pulling in a bit further up.

'Look what I've made,' George, holding up his rocket so Angus could see it.

Rachael wound down the passenger window and Clare leant in.

'That's great George,' she said, admiring the rocket, 'everything OK with you?' she said to Rachael.

'Really good,' said Rachael, smiling.

'That's what I like to hear. Shall I take the boys in?' said Clare.

'If you're sure, that'd be great,' said Rachael, she leant across and opened the door for George to get out.

'I can't wait for an up-date,' said Clare, raising her eyebrows.

'I'll fill you in later,' said Rachael, smiling, as she drove off back home to Duncan.

When she let herself in the front door, she could hear the sound of voices and laughter coming from the sitting room.

To her surprise, sitting on the sofa with a mug of coffee in her hand was Lorna.

'Oh hi,' she said, putting her mug down and getting up to meet Rachael, 'I'm sorry to turn up out of the blue like this but I was passing and saw a light on and lovely Duncan let me in. It's so good to see him again after so long,' she turned and gave him a winning smile.

Rachael felt slightly sick. She flashed straight back to when she had been going out with Duncan years ago and Lorna was always flirting with him. She'd actually had to say to her 'hands off he's mine,' Lorna had laughed but Rachael hadn't found it funny. Now here she was again, up to her old tricks.

'I was just wondering,' said Lorna, looking a bit pathetic, her head on one side, 'if I could stay here for a bit now you're back in the house. The thing is I've nowhere else to go.'

Chapter Forty-eight

Grandad was really worried about Nana. She'd started an awful cold, about ten days ago, streaming nose, eyes watering, the works. And now it had gone down onto her chest. It really hurt him to hear her coughing and watch her familiar lined face all screwed up with pain.

He took her up a cup of hot lemon and honey and put it on the bedside table.

'Here you are sweetheart,' he said.

She began to thank him but as she took an intake of breath, she started one of her coughing fits.

'I think it's time to call the doctor out, love,' he said gravely.

'Oh no, I'm fine,' she wheezed, 'really, it's just a nasty old cough and cold.'

'I think it may be flu,' he said.

'It can't be, we've had our jabs, remember.'

'Yes, but they said on the news that it doesn't cover all the different strains.'

'You watch too much television, you do,' Nana said, 'I tell you what I'd really like, a hot water bottle for my chest.'

'Yes, alright,' he said, 'shall I microwave the one Rachael got you at Christmas?'

'Oh, no, it's not the same as the old rubber one. Can you manage it?'

'Of course I can manage it,' said Grandad, hoping he'd have the strength to screw the lid up tightly enough.

He was finding it more and more difficult these days to open and close bottles and tins. The power just wasn't there. To think what a strong man he'd been in his youth; joining the local gym, lifting weights, putting up tents, rowing, cycling. He always thought his fine physique was one of the things that made her say 'yes' when he proposed.

'But, I am worried about you,' he said, picking up a used tissue from the floor, 'I can't manage without you, you know.'

'Oh don't be silly and cheer up,' said Nana, 'you've got a face like a drink of cold water.'

'I can't help it,' he said 'I hate seeing you like this, it makes me so angry.'

'Please don't be,' said Nana, 'that'll just make it worse.'

She gave a violent sneeze that turned into a painful cough.

'I'll go and get your hottie,' he said, and bid a hasty retreat.

He was always like this if she was ill in bed, Nana thought. He never understood that she needed to see him smile if he popped his head round the door or maybe cheer her up with a little quip. Instead she found herself worrying as much about him as herself. Mind you, he was tired. He wasn't used to going up and down the stairs so often, rustling up something to eat and putting a wash in the machine. She'd had to talk him through every stage of the cycle. It made her realise that she did do most of the household chores, even though he was at home all the time now. She didn't usually mind, that was the way it had always been, but she hated not being able to keep the house in order, now she was poorly. God knows what state the kitchen was in.

She sighed and reached for her hot lemon and another cough erupted, which made her spill her drink down the front of her pin bed-jacket. Bother. Now that would have to go in the wash. She felt like having a little cry, it was the last straw, it really was. Luckily the hot lemon had only been luke warm, so she didn't burn herself.

She must be coming to the end of this cold and cough, surely. Three days to come, three days to stay, and three days to go, her mother used to say. Nearly there, she closed her eyes, she was exhausted by it.

§

Downstairs, Grandad put the kettle on for the hot water bottle and sat in his armchair, to rest for a minute or two while it boiled.

He was suddenly struck by the most massive pain, unlike anything he had ever experienced before. He clutched his chest and took a huge intake of breath.

It turned out to be his last.

Chapter Forty-nine

Rachael was devastated by the death of her father. It was such a shock. She and Lorna had been so worried about Mum, since her heart attack and especially lately, when she couldn't seem to shake off her cold and cough, it had never crossed their minds that it could be Dad who went first.

Apparently poor Mum had waited for ages for him to bring her a hot water bottle, and then called and called, but there was no answer. Eventually she was so worried that she dragged herself out of bed and went downstairs to investigate. Hanging onto the bannister and trying to catch her breath, with a terrible fit of coughing, that made her stop half way down.

When she saw him, slumped over to the side of the arm chair, she said she could tell by his face that he had gone. It was a pale grey colour and his eyes were glassy and unfocussed.

She'd sat by his chair holding his hand for about fifteen minutes, before she felt able to phone Rachael.

Rachael had got in the car and driven straight over.

Her Mum was sitting on a hard chair in the kitchen, in a state of shock.

'He's in the sitting room, love,' she said, her lips hardly moving as she spoke.

'I'll be back in a minute Mum,' Rachael said, giving her a kiss on the cheek, then she went into the sitting room to see her Dad.

Time stood still for her as she looked at him. It couldn't be true. Her Dad, her beloved Dad. She wanted to hug him but found she couldn't. It was as if there was already an invisible barrier between them and he was on the other side of it. Gone. Out of reach.

'Love you Dad,' she said, wiping away tears as she went back into the kitchen to make her Mum a cup of tea.

She tried phoning Lorna who wasn't answering, so she left a message asking her to phone back as soon as possible. It was urgent.

She didn't know what to do next. Was there any point in calling the ambulance when it was clearly too late. She phoned 999 and explained what had happened. They were great and said they would get a doctor to the house as soon as possible and an ambulance would also come in case there was still something they could do.

In the end a doctor she didn't know arrived within about half an hour. Not Mum and Dad's own Dr Mayhew, but a lovely Indian woman doctor who confirmed the state of death and gently took Rachael and her Mum back into the kitchen and talked them through what would happen next.

The doctor cancelled the ambulance call out and arranged with the local funeral parlour for Dad to be taken by them to the mortuary.

They arrived about an hour later and Rachael and her mum went upstairs when they came to collect him. They couldn't bear to watch.

Finally, the house was empty apart from Rachael and her mum.

They sat together in the sitting room, talking quietly. Comfortable in each other's presence, sharing the grief.

Later Lorna phoned, very bubbly.

'Sorry I didn't phone back but I've been on a spa day with my friend Sue, you remember her, very short with red hair. What is it? What's happened? Is Mum alright?'

Rachael broke the news. There was a moment of silence and then Lorna burst into tears.

'Oh no, I can't believe it. Poor Daddy, I didn't even get a chance to say goodbye. How's Mum, shall I come over?'

'Well, why don't you come over to my house a little later,' said Rachael, 'Mum's going to come and stay with me for a few days. We're just going to pack up a few things to bring with her. Her friend next door has offered to look after Torvill and Dean. We'll be leaving in about ten minutes.'

'OK,' said Lorna, 'can I speak to Mum?'

Rachael handed the phone to her mother.

'Lorna wants a quick word,' she said.

Her mother took the phone and Rachael noticed that her hands were shaking.

'Hello Darling.'

'Oh Mum, I'm so sorry about Dad and about everything.'

'It's alright Lorna, don't worry. I can't really speak much now, we'll talk over at Rachael's, shall we?'

They hadn't spoken since Lorna had left the house when she was pregnant.

'I love you, Mum,' said Lorna obviously crying.

'Love you too. I'm so sorry you lost the baby.'

'Thanks Mum.'

'Bye for now,' said her mother and handed the phone back to Rachael.

She had been incredibly hurt that Lorna had contacted Rachael, not her, after losing the baby. And she felt sad that her husband would never see Lorna again, he'd always been stupidly fond of her for all her faults. Still at least she was alive and safe. She really wanted to see her. She must have been through so much pain and heartache. Apparently she had miscarried at five months.

'Come on Mum,' said Rachael, 'let's get you back to my place.'

§

When George was delivered back from football, Rachael knew she had to tell him what had happened.

As soon as he came in he saw Nana in the hall and gave her a great big hug.

'Hello Nana,' he said, 'where's Grandad?'

Rachael took him upstairs to his room and quietly told him that Grandad had suddenly got ill and because he was so old, sadly he had died.

The child got into bed still in his clothes and pulled the blankets up over his head.

'I know it's hard, darling,' Rachael said, 'we all loved Grandad very much.'

'I don't want to talk about it,' said the child said.

'He wasn't in any ….'

'I said I don't want to talk about it, Mummy,' said George, furiously, turning away from her under the covers.

Rachael took a moment.

'Alright, sweetheart,' she said, 'I'll leave you alone for a little. Tea will be ready in a minute, so come down when you want to.'

She quietly left the room, pulling the door to as she went. She put her hand over her mouth. It was so sad. She knew George had really loved his Grandad. This was another trauma in his young life and God knows he'd had enough already.

The child hardly spoke at all during tea or at bedtime. Just went into his room and closed the door.

In the morning, he came in to Rachael and Nana in the kitchen, still in his pyjamas.

'I don't want to go to school' he said, 'and I don't want any breakfast.'

He swiped his cereal bowl off the table and it smashed into pieces all over the floor. He ran back up to his room, slamming the kitchen door behind him.

Rachael and Nana looked at each other.

Dear God, now what?

Chapter Fifty

Visiting time was between two and four and Kate was lying in bed waiting for Tony to arrive.

She was still reeling after her interview with the police that morning.

'It would appear to have been a case of mistaken identity by you and your mother,' the Chief Inspector had said, as he was leaving the room, 'anyway, we'll be back to talk to you again tomorrow morning.'

The moment Tony arrived she burst into tears. He sat on the bed and put his arms round her.

'It's OK, I'm here now,' he said, gently pushing her hair off her face, 'I'm sorry I'm late, we got held up in traffic. So what's the latest, what did the police say?'

She told him everything. She'd never told him before about the rape, she'd always felt it made her seem dirty and used, but now he needed to know, to help make sense of it all.

'You poor cow,' he said, when she'd finished, 'you should have told me before, what a bastard.'

'But the worst thing is the police don't believe me. The man my mother killed, Michael Stanhope, was out of the country the year that I was raped. So now they think I've just made it all up. And what's really scary, is that the man who actually *did* do it, is still out there somewhere, probably doing the same thing to other girls. It's just horrible,' she said, dissolving into tears again.

'What are you going to do when you leave here?' he asked, carefully.

'I don't know, Tony, I've nowhere to go. We left our flat without Mum having paid the rent and I haven't any money anyway.'

Tony took her hand.

'Listen, Dad and I have been talking about it. You must come and stay with us,' he said, 'for the moment anyway, until this mess is sorted out.'

'Oh my God, are you sure,' she said, feeling a massive sense of relief, 'but what about your dad, are you sure he won't mind?'

'He's fine about it,' said Tony, 'he's been quite lonely since Mum died. I think he'd enjoy your company. He's got a bit of a dodgy ticker, so he's retired now. You can look after each other, when I'm working.'

'Well, you'd better double check with him,' she said, 'it's a big ask.'

'Hang on, he's downstairs in the cafe, I'll go and get him and he can tell you himself.'

He gave a kiss on the lips and made for the door.

'Back in a sec,' he said, and went out.

Kate leant back against the pillow She felt utterly drained. It was all too much. She gave a massive shaky sigh and took a sip of water. She had to try and just take each day as it came and not worry about the future.

The door opened after a bit and Tony and his dad came in.

'How are you doing, girl,' said his dad, coming to the side of the bed.

'Not too bad,' she said.

'You're looking a bit peaky,' he said, patting her hand, 'Tony's filled me in on your situation. You'd better come and stay with us for a while, we can fatten you up, eh?'

'Really, are you sure?' said Kate gratefully, 'thank you so much, just for a bi, anyway. I'll try not to be a nuisance.'

'No problem,' he said tersely. He was moved by this girl and the horrors she'd been through. He and his wife had lost Tony's elder sister to meningitis when she was in her first year at university, she'd looked a little like Kate and her room was still empty. It was time there was life in it again. Also he knew that this relationship was important to Tony. He'd already said he wanted to marry Kate when the time was right.

'When will the hospital let you leave?' he asked her.

'Once the doctor has seen me tomorrow, I think. The police are coming first though. They've still got more questions for me. Apparently, they're trying to find somewhere for me to go. I can't stay here any longer because they're really short of beds.'

'Well, tell them they can come and talk to you at our place whenever they want to, I'll contact them and let them know we're going to take care of you,' said Tony's father.

'You're being so kind,' said Kate, feeling near to tears.

'I told you, he likes you,' said Tony.

Kate smiled at them both.

'You've been on the news,' his dad said, 'pictures of the crash and of you being lifted into the ambulance and then arriving at the hospital. God knows how they get these stories out so quickly. The press want to talk to you as well. At the moment they're not being allowed into the hospital. The police have said strictly no visitors. We'll try and work out a back route for us to leave tomorrow.'

Tony looked at his father and realised that he was back into police-mode and enjoying the challenge of being part of it all. Things had been very quiet for him since he'd left the force.

A nurse came in and looked at the watch pinned to her pocket.

'Sorry, I'm going to have to ask you to leave now. Visiting time is nearly over and I need to redo Kate's dressings.'

'Right, all being well, we'll pick you up at two o'clock tomorrow,' Tony's father said.

'Bye,' said Tony, giving her a gentle kiss, 'can't wait for us to be back at our place. And don't worry, it's all going to be alright. You've got us looking after you now.'

They went out as the nurse wheeled in a trolley with dressings on.

'Oh, someone's sent you some flowers,' she said to Kate, 'they've only just been delivered, they're on the desk. I'll bring them in a sec, once we've finished.'

Kate was surprised. Who could be sending her flowers?

Once she'd changed the dressings, mostly cuts and scrapes, and a few stitches on her knee, the nurse bustled out with her trolley and came back a moment later with some red roses.

'There you are, pet,' she said, putting them on the table over the bed, 'I'll try and find a vase for them in a bit.'

As she left the room, Kate opened the small envelope attached to the flowers and took out the typed card.

As she read it, her blood ran cold:

'I know where you are "blue eyes" and I'm coming to get you.'

It was from him.

Chapter Fifty-one

As she rang for the nurse, Kate thought she was going to be sick. All the old fear and panic swept over her. He knew where she was. He was coming to get her.

'What is it love,' said the nurse. She was the new shift; a motherly looking black woman who'd just come on duty.

'Is the hospital locked at night?' Kate asked desperately.

'Why, is someone after you,' the nurse joked with an amused smile.

'Yes, I think they may be,' said Kate, seriously.

'Well, don't you worry, my dear, we will take care of you. Your room is right opposite the nurses station, and the police have given strict instructions that you receive no visitors, apart from your young man and his father and yes, the hospital is locked at night-time, so you're quite safe. Nobody crosses this threshold unless I say so!'

She stood foursquare in the doorway with her arms folded across her chest.

Kate managed a weak smile.

Poor girl, thought the nurse. The staff had all been filled in about the accident. No wonder she was paranoid about bad things happening to her. She made a mental note to suggest to sister that they should give her an extra strong sleeping pill tonight. At least it would give the poor child a chance to rest. She spotted the roses on the bed table.

'Oh, lovely, would you like me to put them in a vase for you?'

'No thanks,' said Kate slamming her good arm on top of them.

'Oh, alright then, maybe later, mmn?' she gave a quizzical look at Kate and left the room, humming.

Kate shoved the flowers and the card into her bedside cupboard, trying to keep calm and decide what to do. Thank God Tony and his dad were collecting her tomorrow. The rapist could have no idea where they lived.

In the morning when the police came, she'd show them the flowers and the card and tell them that the rapist had called her 'blue eyes' when he'd dumped her in the alley. They probably wouldn't believe her, but she had to tell them anyway. Tony would believe her.

She was so scared, she couldn't eat any supper. She spent the whole evening watching the door, with her finger on the green button to call for help if he suddenly appeared. If only she had her mobile she could have phoned Tony. She hadn't even got her Mum to talk to any more.

By the time the nurse came in with the last round of pills, she was in quite a lot of pain with her shoulder having been tensed up all evening, twisting to get a good hold of the emergency button. She would scream loudly if he came and one of the nurses would come before he could hurt her, she kept telling herself.

'Here you are, darling,' said the nurse, handing her pills in a tiny white paper cup, 'you get these down you, and you'll feel much better.'

Within fifteen minutes she was in such a deep sleep that she had no idea of what happened during the night.

Chapter Fifty-two

Nana had been staying with Rachael for five days. She was still pretty unwell. The doctor had given her a prescription of antibiotics for her cough and some sleeping pills to help her cope with the death of her husband. She had been really pleased to see Lorna again and they'd both cried together about the loss of Grandad and of the baby and everything that had happened. Nana was in the spare room and Lorna was sleeping on the sofa.

Grandad dying had eased the tension between Rachael and Lorna but it was still quite difficult.

Duncan had been a great help, driving George to and from school and going with Rachael and Nana to register the death and helping her make all the funeral arrangements. Nana had always liked him when he was going out with Rachael years ago, before he went off to university. So much better than Michael she always thought, although she felt guilty even thinking that now, after the murder, but it was true. There had been something about Michael that she hadn't trusted.

That evening, Rachael, Nana and Lorna were in the sitting room after George had gone to bed.

'I think I'd like to go home tomorrow,' Nana said, 'I think it's time, and Torvill and Dean will be missing me.'

Rachael and Lorna looked at each other. Surely she was too frail to be all by herself after such a big shock.

'Are you sure, Mum,' Rachael said, 'you know you're welcome to stay here as long as you want.'

'I know, darling,' said Nana, 'but I need to get back. It's no good burying my head in the sand, I've got to face up to what's happened and find a way to carry on.'

'You're so brave, Mum,' said Lorna, 'look, why don't I come and live with you for a bit, at least until you're feeling more settled.'

Rachael took a deep breath and looked at her mother to see what the response would be. It was the obvious answer. Lorna had nowhere to live and her mother would be needing company to help her get through all this. She sent up a silent prayer.

'Oh Lorna, I would love that,' said Nana, her face lifting, 'but are you sure. Don't you have other plans?'

'None at all,' said Lorna, smiling ruefully, 'I only wish I did.'

Careful Lorna, don't blow it, thought Rachael.

'Plenty of time,' said Nana, 'someone will come along, you'll see.'

As long as it's not Duncan! Rachael thought.

Next morning, she told George that Nana needed to go home now to sort everything out and that Auntie Lorna was going to go and live with her for a bit to look after her.

'Is Nana going to die now, as well?' he asked, crossly.

'No, darling, Nana's fine, she's just got some jobs to do at home, but we'll go over and see her very soon and maybe she'll make you a special cake.'

'I don't want jam in it', said George.

Chapter Fifty-three

When Kate finally woke in the morning, the effects of the sleeping pill still clouding her mind, she slowly became aware that she was in a different room and that there was a lot of activity going on in the corridor.

She immediately pressed the green call button by her side and after a few minutes, a nurse came hurrying in.

'Oh, good morning,' she said, 'my word, you have had a good long sleep.'

'Why am I in another room?' Kate asked, 'what's happened?'

'Nothing for you to worry about, everything's fine, but there had to be a few changes in the night due to an emergency.'

'What sort of emergency?' asked Kate, her mind full of horrendous possibilities of the rapist turning up, walking silently through the hospital, then creeping into her room during the night.

'Well, you'll see it on the news, I'm sure. There's been a terrorist attack at a local concert. Fourteen dead and lots of people injured. We're one of the receiving hospitals, so of course it's been frantic. We needed your old room opposite the nurses' station, for a young girl who has multiple problems and we had to check her frequently through the night.'

'So where am I now?' said Kate feeling totally disorientated.

'You're in No 16 at the far end of the corridor. But I gather you won't be with us for long. I hear you should be going home today.'

'Yes that's right,' said Kate with a small smile.

Going home with Tony. She couldn't wait. She had been told that the hospital would let her leave with some crutches and one of their wheelchairs. They had to be returned once she'd sorted out some of her own.

'Now then, your breakfast will be here in a minute,' said the nurse, 'it's already seven-thirty, so let's sit you up a bit.'

She carefully helped Kate into a sitting position, and pulled the bed table across her.

'And the police are coming to see you again this morning,' she said, 'we have to get you ready by ten o'clock.'

'Where are my roses?' Kate asked, suddenly. She had to show them to the police, and the card that came with them.

'Your roses?' said the nurse, straightening her covers, 'oh, don't you worry, we'll bring the vase through a bit later.

'No you don't understand, I shoved them into my bedside cupboard,' said Kate trying to look at the one by her bed, but unable to because of the bed tray.

The nurse gave her an odd look and bent down to open it.

'Oh yes, here they are,' she said, reaching in and fishing them out, 'they're a bit worse for wear, I'm afraid.'

'Just leave them, put them back in the cupboard, please,' said Kate getting more and more anxious.

'Did you not want them, love?' said the nurse, sympathetically, 'shall I throw them away for you?' She knew a thing or two about unwanted gifts.

'No, sorry, it's alright,' said Kate, 'just leave them in there.'

'Right you are,' said the nurse putting them back in, aware that the stems were now bent, 'we always transfer the bedside cupboard with the patient if they need to change rooms, so you don't need to worry.'

There was an urgent beeping in the corridor.

'I've got to go now, I'll be back later, alright? Ring your buzzer if you have any problems,' she said, closing the door as she went.

Kate took a moment to get her thoughts together. God that sleeping pill had been strong, she still felt drugged. She couldn't wait to leave the hospital now and have time and peace to work out what was going to happen to her next, what life had in store for her. She had no mother! It was hard to believe, after all those years closeted with her. She supposed that she was now an orphan. But then again maybe not, as her father, whoever he was, might still be alive. She wondered if she would ever be able to track him down. People seemed to be able to these days. She decided to ask Tony to help her find him.

There was a knock on the door and she nearly jumped out of her skin. It was him. The rapist. She put her hand on the buzzer.

The door opened and a cheery little woman popped her head round.

'Here we are, dear - breakfast,' she said, coming in with a tray, pushing the door open with her shoulder.

'Thank you,' said Kate, feeling sick and letting go of the buzzer.

Chapter Fifty-four

As soon as the Chief Inspector entered the room, followed by a detective, Kate handed him the bunch of flowers and the card.

She'd got the nurse to get them out of the cupboard and put them on the bed table as soon as the breakfast tray had been taken.

'They're from him,' she said desperately, 'the rapist. He called me "blue eyes" when he left me on the pavement, I've never forgotten it. Sometimes I still have nightmares where I can hear him saying it, over and over.'

'OK, calm down. You're quite safe. Don't worry, we won't let anything happen to you.'

He motioned to the detective who pulled a plastic bag from his pocket and carefully put the flowers and the card inside, then sealed it.

Kate was surprised, she'd half expected them not to believe her.

'Looks to me as if they've been bought from a roadside seller,' he said to the detective, 'no florist markings and he's typed the card himself, or got someone else to. No hand-writing, of course.'

'Now listen,' he said drawing a chair up to the side of Kate's bed, 'I don't want you to be scared, but there have been some developments.'

Kate immediately felt a chill run through her. This didn't sound good.

'After our talk yesterday, in the hope of verifying at least part of your story, we ran some tests to establish if there had been any similar incidents in Bromley during the summer you told us you were attacked. It turns out that there were indeed three other cases of rape in the vicinity and due to the evidence of two of the girls we were able to arrest the man responsible and take him to court. He was found guilty and sentenced to seven years in prison.'

'Good,' said Kate.

'Now, whether this was your attacker or not, needs to be confirmed,' he took from his brief-case a black and white photo, put it on the bed table and slid it towards her, 'take a look.'

Kate stared at the photo, it was so similar to Michael Stanhope, it could have been him. She gasped and then retched with her hand over her mouth.

'I'm sorry,' she said, tears blurring her eyes, 'it's him. Oh my God. Where is he now, is he out of jail, he must be, to have sent me the flowers, is he here, somewhere nearby?'

She was really frightened. After all this time, he had come to get her. It was what she had always feared.

'Now, don't jump to conclusions. Even if the flowers were from him, he might have got someone else to deliver them. Anyway he won't turn up here today, the hospital is crawling with police after a terrorist attack last night at a local concert.'

'Yes, I heard,' said Kate shakily, 'it's so awful.'

'And in a couple of hours,' he went on, 'your boyfriend is coming to pick you up and you'll be out of harm's way. The man will have no way of knowing where you are.'

'So he's actually out of jail, just wandering around free to do it again,' said Kate. She was aware that she was beginning to sound a bit hysterical and took some deep breaths to try and calm down.

'He's out on parole, at the moment.'

'What does that mean?' asked Kate.

'That he's still being closely monitored. If he gets in any trouble he'll go straight back inside. The two girls who took him to court were prepared, before he was released, but of course we had no knowledge of your case so we weren't able to warn you. He's been banned from being within a twenty mile radius of Bromley, where both the girls live. Again, if he breaks that order he'll be sent straight back to jail.'

'Is there anything I can do? I'm sure he'll try and find me, wherever I go.' Kate said, panicking.

'You'll be given an immediate response number to call if you see any sight of him but I think it's extremely unlikely.'

'How did he know I was here?' Kate asked.

'The crash was in the papers and there were photos of you and your mother printed, alongside all the details of Michael Stanhope's murder. He must have seen it and recognised you.'

'Am I under suspicion of anything?' asked Kate, fearfully.

'No, we've eliminated you from our enquiries, you'll be glad to hear,' the Chief Inspector said with a small smile, 'the one thing that has been made clear now, is your mother's motive for killing Michael Stanhope. So that in itself is progress.'

He stood up and moved the chair back to wall.

'We'll leave you now and be in touch if there's any further news.'

'Don't go,' said Kate, not wanting to be alone, waiting for Tony to arrive.

'I'm sorry, I'm afraid we have to get on. To put your mind at rest, I'll arrange for one of the hospital security guards to sit outside your door until you're collected, alright?'

'Thank you,' said Kate feeling suddenly weepy. She grabbed a tissue and blew her nose.

'No problem,' said the Chief Inspector, shaking her hand, 'good luck.'

They left the room closing the door behind them.

'Poor kid,' he said to his colleague, as they walked down the corridor, 'she's had a tough ride.'

Chapter Fifty-five

Now that Nana and Lorna had gone, Rachael was just beginning to feel a bit calmer, when she received a frantic call from Clare.

'Oh, Rachael, thank God you're in,' she said.

'What is it, what's happened?'

'It's Finn, he's coming here and he wants to take Angus.'

'What do you mean? He can't just come and take him,' said Rachael.

She'd never met Clare's husband, but she hadn't much liked the sound of him when Clare talked about him. A man very obsessed with himself and his own achievements. Living in Scotland, she remembered. A mountain climber or something.

'Apparently, he and his girlfriend have come up with the idea that it would be great for Angus to spend half-term with them,' Clare went on, 'that it would be a chance for him to have some quality time with Finn and get to know his girlfriend and her son. He wants to collect Angus tonight and take him straight back up to Scotland with him. He's on his way to us, now.'

'Tonight?' said Rachael, 'that's a bit sudden. What does Angus think?'

'That's the problem, he really doesn't want to go,' said Clare sounding very worried, 'he hasn't seen Finn for ages and he hasn't even met this woman or her son. I mean, I do feel guilty that I've had Angus the whole time since we split, and Finn is his father after all, but this is just too out of the blue and I don't think it'd be right for Angus. He wouldn't be getting Finn to himself and he might not like this woman or her son.'

'Did you tell Finn how he felt?' said Rachael.

'I didn't get the chance,' said Clare, 'he just said to pack a bag for Angus and he'd be with us in a couple of hours, then rang off. I tried to phone him back but he didn't answer the call.'

'What are you going to do?' asked Rachael.

'Do you think we could possibly come and stay with you for a couple nights,' said Clare, 'until this is sorted. Finn doesn't know who you are or where you live, so all he could do is speak to me on my mobile and that would give us a chance to talk the idea through logically and sensibly. I mean I don't want him to arrive on the doorstep and for us to have a big scene in front of Angus.

'Of course you can come,' said Rachael, seeing the prospect of a peaceful evening slipping away, 'George will be thrilled to have Angus here, you can stay as long as you need. Hurry on over and don't take too long, in case he arrives earlier than expected.'

'I know, I'll get to you as soon as possible. Thank you so much, Rachael,' she said, and rang off.

It was the least she could do, Rachael thought. Clare had been such a fantastic support for her during the murder case. But now all her plans were up in the air. Duncan was supposed to be coming round at 7 o'clock, she'd planned a special meal and they were going to snuggle in and watch something on Netflix after George had gone to bed. She sighed, she'd better phone him and cancel. She could see Clare was going to need to talk it all through with her and the house would be chaotic with the two boys rushing around.

She hoped Finn didn't turn nasty, when he arrived at Clare's house and found she and Angus weren't there. Especially if he'd come all the way from Scotland.

It wasn't really the best time for her to have them to stay. Next week was going to be really fraught. She had the surveyor coming round on Monday for her house buyer and then her dad's funeral on the Wednesday. She'd half wondered if she should let George come to it, he'd really loved his Grandad, but then she'd decided that he was too young. It would be disturbing for him and he'd hate to see her and Nana and Lorna all upset. Clare had already said she'd have George for the day and they'd do something special as it was half-term, maybe go to the cinema.

But now that there was this new problem with Finn. Who knew what was going to happen. If it escalated and Clare couldn't have George on Wednesday, maybe Duncan could step in.

She phoned him and explained and he was fine about it all. Said it was no problem, and to give him a ring in a day or two. Then she went upstairs and told George, who was thrilled Angus was coming for a sleepover and started wildly fighting round his bedroom with his Star Wars lightsaber. Angus would have to share George's bed. It would be a squash but they'd manage. She made up the folding bed in the box room for Clare and moved the airer with the damp clothes on, out into the hall.

Poor Clare, she thought, how tricky it was for her. If Angus didn't want to go with his father, and Finn insisted, it could cause all sorts of problems and upsets.

Her head was spinning with it all but before she could find any words of wisdom to give her, the doorbell rang.

They'd arrived.

Chapter Fifty-six

The Rapist sat on the bed in the B&B near the hospital. He didn't mind the small size of the room, it was like being back in his cell. Almost comforting in a strange way.

So he'd missed her, damn it. When he'd enquired by phone mid afternoon about how she was, saying he was family, he was told that she'd already left. And no, they had no idea where she would be going.

He couldn't believe it. He had been so close. When he saw her photo in paper he recognised her at once and remembered her soft yielding flesh as he went about his business. He wanted to see her one more time. He felt it was his right. She was one of his, he had taken her and so he part-owned her.

After sending the flowers yesterday, he had planned to slip into the hospital before it was closed for the night and find her room. It wouldn't take him long. If she was alone he might put his hand over her mouth and give her a repeat performance. She would only be wearing a nightie after all. It wouldn't take long.

Night after night in prison, he'd gone over the rapes that he had committed, in fine detail, working out how to improve his activities once he was out. He knew he couldn't stop, it was a central part of who he was and what he needed.

It had been easy enough to convince the prison psychologists and the parole board that he was truly sorry and that he would never do it again. He was a model prisoner. He had talks with the visiting pastor and said he was a believer and that he was ashamed of what he'd done. The man of the cloth had said that if he was truly repentant, God would forgive him. After that they sort of left him alone, to see out his sentence.

The first thing he wanted to do on release was to see if he could find each of his victims. See how they were getting on and maybe pay them a call. Especially the two bitches who had taken him to court and got him convicted. He would make them pay big-time.

He was furious and frustrated that a condition of his parole was that he was not allowed within a twenty-five mile radius of Bromley, where each of them lived and which used to be his stamping ground. Most of his carefully planned attacks had happened within the banned area.

But the hospital was not. So even if he was apprehended by the police, he would not be breaking his parole. And they had no idea that Kate was one of his victims as her name had never come up in his court case. He knew girls who had been raped, often didn't report it to the police, unable to face the humiliation of a trial and feeling they'd somehow brought it on themselves. Which in his mind, they had, with their short skirts and low tops. Driving men mad with lust but forbidden to touch. What did they expect?

He'd felt a mounting excitement as he approached the hospital on his mission, only to find a scene of utter chaos when he got there. Blue lights, ambulances, people being rushed in on gurneys, and armed police everywhere. What the hell was going on? Could only be some sort of terrorist attack.

There was no way he was going into that maelstrom, he'd be questioned and arrested before he'd got through the doors. He walked calmly and quietly on past the hospital gates as if going somewhere else and then doubled back to the B&B by a different route. His visit to Kate would have to wait a day or two.

And now this. She'd gone. He'd bloody missed her.

He'd been feeling very unsettled since his release. He didn't know how to start again, build a new life for himself. He had a bit of money put by and realised he'd have to sell his Bromley flat and re-locate somewhere. Hopefully it had gone up in price while he'd been away.

His few friends had dropped off like flies when the details of his rape case came out in the press, as had his adoptive parents who'd never really wanted him anyway. No son of ours, was their response when interviewed by reporters.

He began to feel the urge for sex. It had been eight long years since he'd had any. He stood up and checked himself in the mirror above the basin. Not too bad.

He decided to get himself to the nearest night club and see what he could find.

Chapter Fifty-seven

About half an hour after Clare and Angus had arrived, Clare's mobile rang. It was Finn. He was furious that they weren't at the house when he got there.

The boys were playing upstairs and Clare put the phone on loudspeaker so Rachael could hear.

'I'm sorry Finn,' Clare said into the phone, 'but Angus doesn't want to come, it's too sudden. Why didn't you phone before you set off and tell me what you were planning?'

'Because I knew you'd react like this and I wanted to surprise Angus before you put a damper on the whole idea,' said Finn.

'I think he'd love it up there and this half-term is the perfect opportunity for him to come and meet Sarah and Christopher.'

'You don't get it, do you?' Clare said angrily, 'he hasn't seen you for months, he's never met your girlfriend or her son, and he's settled where he is. He doesn't want to come, Finn.'

'You mean you don't want him to come,' he retorted.

'Look, you were supposed to visit us in the summer and spend the afternoon with him, but you cried off at the last minute and he was really disappointed.'

'That wasn't my fault,' he said.

'It never is, Finn.'

'You stupid woman, it was an important business meeting about the Pennines walk. I had to go.'

'Of course you did,' said Clare, sarcastically.

Rachael could see the red flush on Clare's chest rising up her neck.

'He's my son Clare, as much as yours. You can't stop me seeing him. I could just come and take him, you know?' he shouted, angrily.

'Yeah, and I could take you to court.'

She looked over at Rachael, who went over to shut the door, in case the boys heard.

'Thanks?' Clare said to her, holding the phone away from her mouth.

'Have you got someone there with you?' asked Finn, sharply.

'Only a friend,' said Clare.

'What's his name, do I know him?'

'It's a her and no you don't,' said Clare.

'Well, I'm here now. Are you going to let me see Angus or not?'

Clare sighed.

'Not tonight,' she said, 'it's too late and he's tired after football.'

'Well, ask him again. I've already booked seats for us on the train tonight and it would be a great adventure for him. I'll come and pick him up, just tell me where you are.'

'Finn, it would be too much for him. Just leave it for now and come and see him next time you're in London.'

'You molly-coddle him, Clare, you always have done.'

'He's a sensitive boy, Finn, and he's still quite shy with strangers.'

'Do you think I don't know that - he's my son! I wouldn't have suggested this if I didn't think he could handle it.'

'I'm sorry Finn, I'm not going to change my mind,' Clare said, 'phone me when you're back in Scotland and we can talk about it again. Maybe we could arrange for him come and stay with you next Easter if he wants to. That'll give him a bit of time to get used to the idea.'

'OK you win,' said Finn angrily, 'but I think you're making a big mistake. I can't believe you can be so selfish. I've had a hell of a day with three charity meetings dealing with obstinate fools… and now this. You're ruining my plans to see my own son.'

'Bye Finn,' said Clare, firmly and ended the call. It rang again almost immediately and she turned the phone off.

'Oh God,' she said to Rachael, 'I don't think I handled that very well.'

'You did fine,' said Rachael, hating to see her cool calm friend in such an upset state.

'The trouble is he's used to getting his own way,' Clare went on, 'he comes up with an idea and assumes everyone will do what he wants. That's the way he was when I was with him. He finds it hard to see someone else's point of view, he just rides over it.'

'Do you want a cup of tea?' asked Rachael.

'Oh yes, I'd love one,' said Clare, gratefully.

'Maybe by next Easter he'll change his mind,' said Rachael, as they made their way through to the kitchen.

'Yes, or get a two year job in Alaska or somewhere. Another amazing opportunity that he can't turn down!' said Clare wryly.

'Well, that would solve your problem,' said Rachael giving her a hug.

Clare laughed.

'Thanks,' she said.

Chapter Fifty-eight

When they heard Rachael coming over to close the door, George and Angus raced quickly upstairs. They'd been in the hall, listening and they'd heard most of the conversation.

'What's going on?' asked George curiously, once they were back in his bedroom.

'It's my Daddy,' said Angus, 'he wants me to go and live with him, Mummy told me in the car.'

'In Scotland?'

'Yes.'

'Do you want to?'

'Not really,' said Angus, frowning, 'he's got a new girlfriend and I hate her.'

'Have you met her?'

'No,' said Angus.

'Then how do you know you hate her?'

'I just do.'

The child thought about this for a moment.

'I don't want you to go,' he said.

'Neither do I,' said Angus, frowning.

'Don't you love your Daddy?'

'He's alright,' said Angus, 'but he likes his girlfriend's little boy better than me, because he lives with him all the time and he hardly ever comes to see me.'

'He said on the phone that he could just come and take you,' said George, worried.

'I know,' said Angus, biting his thumb nail.

'Do you think he might kidnap you?' asked George.

'Probably,' said Angus crossly, punching the pillow on George's bed.

'He sounded very angry,' said George, 'are you scared?'

'No,' said Angus, defensively, 'but Mummy will be sad if I go away.'

'What about me,' said George, 'who will I play with?'

'One of the other boys from school, I expect,' said Angus.

'I don't like any of them,' said George, 'they're stupid.'

'If I go with him, he might not bring me back.' said Angus.

'You're bleeding,' said George.

'Oh, yes,' said Angus looking at his thumb where he'd bitten off a bit of skin by his nail. He sucked his thumb and then started biting the nail again.

'I've got an idea.' said George, suddenly.

'What?' said Angus.

'We could run away,' said George, inspired, 'then he can't take you with him, can he?'

'No,' said Angus and started to laugh.

George began laughing too and they started rolling around on the bed, chanting 'run away, run away, run away.'

'Where shall we go?' asked Angus, as they stopped and caught their breath.

'We can build a camp house in the woods, like Bear Grylls,' said George.

'I don't like bears,' said Angus, suddenly a bit nervous.

'No, he's a man who lives in a forest, haven't you seen him on television?'

'No,' said Angus.

'He's amazing,' said George, 'anyway, there aren't any bears in England.'

'There are in the zoo,' said Angus knowledgeably.

'Do you want to run away or not?' asked George, impatiently.

Angus thought about it.

'Yes,' he said, 'when shall we go?'

'Straight after bed-time, once they think we're asleep. We'll stuff some clothes in the bed, so it'll look as if we're still there.'

'That's brilliant,' said Angus, clapping his hands, excitedly.

'Yes,' said George modestly. He'd been reading a level three adventure book and the boy in the story had done that.

'Boys, supper's ready,' Rachael's voice came up the stairs.

'Come on,' said George, 'and lets bring some food up to take with us tonight.'

'OK,' said Angus.

He thought George was great.

Chapter Fifty-nine

The child and Angus were besides themselves with excitement. They'd packed their school bags with things they thought they might need. Cheese triangles and apples from the kitchen, some sweets that Angus had bought with his pocket money, two tins of diet coke and a torch. They hid the bags under George's bed and lay on it, giggling, fully dressed in their clothes, with their pyjamas on top.

'When are we coming back?' asked Angus.

'Never,' said George, triumphantly.

'What about Mummy,' said Angus, nervously, 'won't she be worried about me?'

'Tell you what,' said George, 'we'll leave them a note, saying we've run away and that we're fine.'

'Yes, and I can draw a picture of us laughing,' said Angus, 'with smoke coming out of our ears!'

George thought this was hysterical and they both doubled up with laughter.

'What are you two up to, in there?' came Rachael's voice from the stairs, 'try to get some sleep both of you.'

'Alright Mummy,' George called, 'sorry.'

They had another fit of the giggles.

They crept out of bed and tore a page out of one of George's school books. Using the light from the hall, George wrote the note and Angus drew the picture on the bottom of it. Then Angus added smoke coming out of George's bottom as well and that set them off laughing all over again.

'Ssshhhh,' said George, 'Mummy's coming, quick get into bed and pretend to be asleep.'

Both of them jumped under the covers and George hid the note under his pillow.

They could hear Rachael's footsteps coming upstairs and along the landing.

'Everything alright, boys?' she asked, blocking the light from the doorway and looking in.

They didn't answer.

After a moment or two they heard her going back down stairs.

'Mummy might come in and kiss me goodnight,' whispered Angus.

'Well, we'll wait a bit longer, then' said George, 'until we can hear them watching TV.'

'OK' said Angus, giving a big yawn.

George lay there, trying hard to keep awake.

It was beginning to get dark and the idea of the woods didn't seem to be so good anyway, not at night. Maybe it would better to wait until the morning and then they could slip out early before Mummy and Clare were awake. They could take a whole packet of custard creams with them from the cupboard. He turned over to tell Angus of the new plan.

Angus was fast asleep.

§

Rachael and Clare shared a bottle of wine and chatted away all evening before finally going up to bed at about midnight.

They looked in at the boys on the way and both of them were fast asleep. Angus up by the pillows and George spread over the rest of the bed.

In the morning, the boys were gone.

Chapter Sixty

Kate was sitting on the sofa rubbing arnica cream into her stump. It had been badly bruised in the crash. Her shoulder was still really painful, but she could feel she was basically on the mend.

She was feeling a bit sorry for herself. Tony was at work and his Dad had gone to the supermarket, so she was on her own for once. Most of the time she was able to keep positive but occasionally things got on top her. Especially now she knew the rapist was out there somewhere looking for her. She felt convinced she would never get rid of him and that one day he would find her again. It was giving her nightmares.

The best thing in her life at the moment was Tony. He'd asked her to marry him and she did love him, although she wasn't really sure he was 'the one'. She was a bit worried that he'd only asked her out of pity. But he wasn't having any of it. 'Look, I've found you and I'm going to look after you', he'd told her. So she'd said 'yes'. She asked if they could wait a bit before getting married. She didn't feel strong enough to take on another momentous event just yet. He totally understood. 'You just let me know when you're ready and we'll do it', he'd said.

Tony's dad had a friend who made prosthetics for soldiers who had lost limbs. He'd contacted the guy who'd said he'd have a look at Kate and see what could be done for her. Although she was grateful for the input, half of her didn't want to go back to all that. The fittings, the visits, the painful attempts at walking hanging on to those bloody rails. The false leg they'd eventually made for her was never comfortable. They kept saying, 'use it as much as you can and you'll get used to it'. But it gave her blisters and made her cry with pain and frustration. In the end her mother had taken the wretched thing from her and thrown it in the bin. 'You're better off without it Kate', she'd said. 'We'll manage. You've got your crutches and the wheelchair, you'll be alright.'

And she had been, up to a point. Life continued and she got stronger, but she still felt sad at all the things she was missing out on. Like dancing and clubbing, and going shopping on her own. She'd still been able to swim, but she always felt people were staring at her stump. Which they were. So she'd only gone a few times before giving up. Also, it had been too much hassle for her mum getting her there and back each time.

She wished that there was a way of making her stump more attractive, she thought, as she ran her hands over it. More solid, like a strong muscle. There was a flabbiness about it which she hated. Maybe she should get it tattooed! There was a thought. It made her smile and she spent the next hour working out possible designs. Some of them very graphic.

Of course, if she was able to get a new limb which she could wear without too much discomfort and which looked attractive and like the other leg, it would change her life beyond all recognition. She might begin to feel part of the human race again. She hardly dared dream it would be possible. She had no money after all, but Tony's dad had said 'leave it with me', and he had a way of making things happen, so who knew? Maybe.

If she did have a chance of getting a new leg, she would love to walk down the aisle. She fantasized about how she would look. Hair swept up, a tiara, a stunning long white dress. She'd have to have a special ivory satin shoe attached to the end of the prosthetic. She couldn't very well have a comfy old sneaker peeping out. She laughed at the thought.

By the time Tony's Dad got back from the supermarket, she had cheered up and was painting her nails.

'You alright, love?' he asked when he got in.

'I'm fine,' she said giving him a big smile.

And she was.

§

That night, the phone rang about half an hour after Tony got back from work.

'It's for Kate,' his dad said, 'it's the Chief Inspector.'

Kate felt her stomach turn over. Now what? She took the phone from him.

'Hello,' she said nervously.

'Is that Kate?' he asked, all business.

'Yes it is,' she answered, feeling even more apprehensive.

'I wonder if I could drop by for a short visit tomorrow morning at ten o'clock. I have some good news for you.'

'Oh yes, of course you can,' said Kate, 'what is it about?'

'I'll tell you tomorrow,' he said and rang off.

Chapter Sixty-one

The following morning, at ten o'clock exactly, the doorbell rang.

Kate had made an effort to look nice. Put on a bit of make up and chosen a pretty top to wear with her jeans. She somehow felt the Chief Inspector would take her more seriously if she looked good. More of a woman and less of a victim.

Tony answered the door and showed him and his side-kick through into the living room, where Kate was waiting, sitting in the armchair.

'Good to see you again,' he said to her, shaking her hand quite formally and choosing to sit on the hard chair, which he brought in towards her.

'Now,' he said, 'you'll be pleased to hear that your attacker is back behind bars.'

'Why, what happened? I've been so worried that he'd find me.'

'Well, you can put your mind at rest,' said the Chief Inspector, referring to his note-book, 'the night of the terrorist attack, he was, as we thought, in the vicinity of the hospital, and took it upon himself to visit one of the local nightclubs. He somehow managed to slip something into a girl's drink and when she started to feel dizzy, he took her outside for some air and attempted to rape her in a nearby alley. What he hadn't bargained for, was that her brother and his rugby-playing friend, came looking for her within minutes. They found them in the alley, caught him on camera in the middle of the attack and called the police. They kept him there in a choke tackle until the patrol car arrived. He was arrested immediately.' He flipped his note-book shut.

'He'd broken his parole of course,' he went on, 'and we now have hard evidence against him for when the girl takes him to court, which she's agreed to do. He won't be allowed out on bail before his case is heard, the judges have little time for re-offenders, and he'll receive a hefty sentence. Particularly as we have another couple of accusations pending, including yours, which we will have time to firm up before his trial. I don't think you'll need to worry about him for a long time.'

Kate let out a long breath. She realised that she'd been holding it in the whole time he was speaking.

'Is the girl alright?' she asked.

'Well, she's still very upset of course but she has strong family support.'

'Oh good,' said Kate, thinking of her mum.

'Thank you so much for telling me,' she went on, 'it's such a relief.'

'All part of the service,' said the Chief Inspector, 'I wanted to let you know before you read about it in the papers. Of course I'll be in touch if there are any further developments. In the meantime, I hope you make a swift recovery from your injuries.'

He got to his feet and he and the detective made for the door.

'Don't worry, we can see ourselves out,' he said.

Within seconds they heard the front door close and they were gone.

Kate turned to Tony and his Dad with a broad smile on her face.

'He's back in jail!' she said, 'I can't believe it.'

'It's fantastic news,' said Tony coming over and giving her a big hug.

'Serves the bugger right,' said Tony's dad, and went off to the kitchen to find some champagne, left over from his retirement party.

Chapter Sixty-two

George and Angus had snuck out of the back door just as it was getting light.

They arrived at the entrance to the park, having run most of the way. It hadn't taken them more than ten minutes but they were out of breath and laughing with the sheer exhilaration of their adventure.

'Come on,' said George, 'let's get over to the woods, then we can hide and start making our camp.'

'What are we going to make it with?' asked Angus, as they crossed a large expanse of grass. He noticed his trainers were getting wet and he could feel damp in his socks.

'Branches,' answered George knowledgeably, 'we just yank them off and make a sort of tent with of them.'

'Right,' said Angus, not fully convinced.

They got to the edge of the trees and started to weave their way past some bushes and on further into the woods.

Suddenly they came to a small clearing, and saw that there was an unshaven man in a bobble hat, lying in a sleeping bag with a dirty blanket on top. There were about four empty cans of beer near him, lying on their side and the remains of old sandwiches scattered about.

He heard them coming and sat up, glaring at them and shaking his fist.

'Pissh off,' he shouted and sort of snarled at them.

George fingered Grandad's knife in his pocket, ready to open it and attack him if he had to.

Then the man started to climb out of his sleeping bag. He was huge.

'What you got in them back-packs?' he slurred, staggering towards them.

'RUN!' shouted George to Angus and they turned back the way they'd come and sprinted as fast as they could through the trees, until they got to the open grass.

'Is he following us?' said Angus, gasping for breath.

'I don't think so,' said George, listening for any sound of him. But it was all quiet except for the birds.

'What are we going to do now?' Angus asked, not sure this was such a good idea after all.

George thought for a moment.

'Let's go and play on the swings,' he said, spotting the children's playground over the other side of the park.

'Yes,' Angus agreed at once.

They ran across the grass, racing each other.

It was still early and the playground was empty, so they had it all to themselves. They dumped their back-packs on the bench and each took one of the big swings. They started going really high, and laughing with the fun of it and the relief of getting away from the man.

Next they went on the roundabout and George was pushing it faster and faster, while Angus was hanging on tightly to one of the rails.

'Stop, stop,' he screamed, half-laughing, 'I'm going to be sick.'

George jumped on as well and on it went, round and round, with the park spinning in front of their eyes. As it eventually began to slow down Angus jumped off with a big leap, fell over and landed heavily on his right knee.

'Did you hurt yourself?' George asked, jumping off as well and going to help him up.

'Only a bit,' said Angus bravely. His knee was bleeding, he felt dizzy and he'd scraped his hand.

'Don't cry,' said George.

'I'm not,' said Angus, wiping a tear with his muddy hand.

'You've got a dirty face now, like in the army,' said George, he scooped up a bit of damp mud from the ground and smeared it on his own face.

'So have you,' said Angus, looking at him and laughing a bit, 'I hurt my knee,' he went on, pushing up his trouser leg.

'Let's have a look,' said George.

They both peered at it.

'It's only bleeding a bit,' George said dismissively.

'It's alright, it doesn't hurt,' said Angus, defensively.

'Good,' said George.

They high-fived.

'Ow,' said Angus.

'What?'

'I scratched my hand too,' he peered down at it.

'Don't be such a baby,' said George.

Angus looked at him. Sometimes he didn't like him very much.

'What shall we do now?' said George, glancing around, 'I know, let's have our picnic!'

'Yes,' said Angus, he was really hungry. They'd crept out of the house without having any breakfast.

They went over to the bench, and sat one each end. Then took the food they'd taken from the kitchen out of their back-packs, and laid it out between them.

'Just a minute,' said George, 'do you want to see a secret?'

'Yes please,' said Angus.

George slowly took Grandad's knife out of his pocket, stroked the shiny dark red handle and then flicked it open.

'Wow,' said Angus, his eyes wide.

'Look,' said George, 'it's really sharp.' He brought the knife down hard into one of the apples and held it aloft, the apple still on the end.

'Goal,' he shouted.

Angus clapped.

'Where did you get it?' he asked.

'It's a secret. You must never tell anyone about it, promise?' said George, 'otherwise…' he drew a finger across his throat.

'Promise,' agreed Angus, a bit frightened.

'Right. Let's eat,' said George, matter of factly, pulling the knife out of the apple, folding it and slipping it back in his pocket.

'Ready, Steady, Go,' he said.

As they started on the picnic, disaster struck.

It started to rain.

Chapter Sixty-three

In the end it was Duncan who found them. Rachael had phoned him, at seven a.m. desperately worried.

'The boys have gone,' she said, in a complete panic.

She told him that she and Clare had woken up to find the two of them missing and then filled him in about Finn wanting to take Angus back to Scotland and that he didn't want to go.

'Do you think Finn could have broken in during the night and kidnapped them?' she said, hysterically.

'Hey, calm down, Rachael,' he said, 'I'm sure he didn't and anyway, why would he take George as well?'

'That's true,' said Rachael, 'oh God, what should we do, Duncan, we've looked everywhere, we can't find them. Should we call the police?'

'Not yet sweetheart,' he said, 'they could just be hiding somewhere and playing a joke on you. You know what kids are like.'

He could hear Clare shouting something.

'Hang on,' Rachael said. After a moment she came back and told him Clare had found a note on the kitchen floor. She read it out to him.

'*We've run away. Don't worry about us we'll be fine,* they've drawn a picture of them with a balloon above Angus' head saying *I don't want to go to Scotland* and one above George saying *neither do I, ha ha.*'

'Well at least they've not been kidnapped!' said Duncan, smiling, 'look, don't panic, they won't have got far. Tell you what, I'll hop in the car and drive round a bit near yours, and see if I come across them. One of you should stay in the house, in case they turn up.'

'Yes, I'll stay here,' Rachael said, 'thanks Duncan. Clare's going to look round the back of the houses. They left the kitchen door and back gate unlocked, so they must have gone out that way.'

'OK,' he said, 'I'll come straight over and start looking.'

He threw on some clothes and went out to the car, grabbing a couple of bags of crisps from the cupboard on the way, in case they were hungry.

He'd hated hearing Rachael so upset on the phone but he loved her all the more for it. She was the one for him, there was no doubt about it. He'd let her slip through his fingers once before and he vowed never to let it happen again. He'd been desolate when he'd learned that she was marrying Michael Stanhope. He should have come back and fought for her but he was too young and inexperienced to know how to do it. He was hurt that she'd chosen someone else. And now there was George. The poor boy had been through so much. He resolved to be there for him, make sure he was alright.

'Where would the boys go?' he asked himself, as he set off through the morning traffic. They probably didn't have any money, unless they'd taken some from Rachael's purse. Would they get on a bus? Unlikely he thought, they wouldn't know where to get off. They wouldn't go to Clare's house in case they ran into Finn. Well, he'd start from near Rachael's home and drive round the local streets in the hope of spotting them.

As he was about half-way there he passed a park on his left.

Yes. That was a distinct possibility. He parked the car up the road and ran back to the gates. The park was pretty empty. Just a man walking his dog. He looked over at the wooded bit and hoped the boys hadn't gone into the trees, to hide. Then something caught his eye, right over the far side of the grass. It was the sun glistening off a spinning roundabout in the kids playground. Eureka, he thought, setting off at a steady jog. Oh great, now it was raining. He pulled up the hood of his sweatshirt and kept going.

When he got to the playground there was no sign of them. Damn, had he missed them? Then he heard voices coming from under the wooden base of the climbing structure. He strode over and peered in.

There they were. Huddled together, with muddy faces and soaking wet, with bits of damp food all round them.

'Oh, hi boys,' he said casually, 'what are you doing here?'

'Just playing,' said George, wiping his face, leaving a chocolate smear.

'Got a bit wet, did you?' Duncan asked.

'Yes,' said Angus 'and our food got spoilt.'

'Hey, that's bad luck,' said Duncan, 'do you want some crisps?'

'Yes, please,' they both said eagerly.

Duncan fished the packets out of his pockets and threw one to each of them.

'Thanks, Duncan,' said George catching his crisps.

'Yes, thanks,' said Angus missing his and picking the bag up off the ground and pulling it open.

Duncan climbed in, crouching over, and sat on the ground with them.

'You've hurt your knee Angus,' he said, 'did you fall off the swing?'

'No, the roundabout,' said Angus, beginning to cry a little. It really did hurt. He'd pushed his trouser leg up again to have another look and he could see there was blood trickling down his shin.

'Do you think we should go back and let Mummy have a look at that and put a plaster on it?'

This was the moment of truth, thought Duncan. They might just say no and go running off.

Angus thought of his Mummy.

'Yes,' he said shakily. He looked at George, who shrugged his shoulders.

They could run away some other time, George thought, it wasn't as much fun as he thought it would be, anyway.

'But what about your Dad?' he asked Angus, suddenly. Remembering why they were running away in the first place. 'Oh, he's not there,' Duncan broke in quickly, 'he had to go back to Scotland last night for important business, so he couldn't stay I'm afraid. Sorry about that Angus.'

'Oh, that's alright,' said Angus, sharing a look of relief with George.

'Come on, then let's go home,' said Duncan, beginning to climb out, his back was killing him, 'look, the rain's stopped. Do you want one more go on the swings?'

'Yes,' they both shouted and raced over to them.

'Bet I can go higher,' said George.

'Bet you can't,' said Angus, forgetting about his knee.

Duncan collected up the wet remains of their picnic and phoned Rachael.

'Duncan?' came her frantic voice over the phone.

'I've found them,' he said, 'they'd gone to the park, they're alive and well.'

'Oh thank God,' said Rachael, 'they're OK,' she shouted to Clare, who'd just got back from a second trip out checking all the gardens.

'Be with you as soon as we can,' said Duncan.

'Thank you so much, love you,' said Rachael, hanging up.

Love you too, girl, thought Duncan.

Chapter Sixty-four

Rachael sat in the middle of the sitting room, surrounded by packing cases. She'd finally managed to exchange contracts on the house and now had only three weeks before completion, when she and George would have to leave.

She'd been convinced that her buyer would drop out at the last moment and had decided not to lift a finger until it was absolutely certain. She'd already had one man who changed his mind, after five weeks of persistent interest, having got surveyors round and everything and she'd found the whole roller coaster of emotions utterly draining.

But now she was in a panic. How the hell was she going to be ready in time. She couldn't believe they had so much stuff. Clare had been great and come over a few mornings to help and Duncan had turned up most evenings, after work. Although by the time they'd eaten and had a few glasses of wine, not a lot of packing had gone on.

Things were going really well between them. He'd given notice on his flat and they'd found an unfurnished house to rent which was quite close to George's school. It wasn't ideal but it would do for the next six months or so, until they found something they might want to buy. That was the plan, anyway. It would also give them a chance to see how they got on, living with each other twenty-four seven, before finally committing to buying a house together but she was pretty sure it was going to be good.

She couldn't believe her luck, that he had found her again and that he still loved her and wanted to be with her. And since he'd discovered the boys in the park, after their great adventure, George had seemed much happier to have him around. She felt they'd established a stronger bond, and she was hopeful that it would work out OK when Duncan was living with them in the new house.

As she looked at the part of the floor where she had found Michael, with his wrists slashed and blood seeping from his stab wounds, she thought she could see the faintest blush of pink rising up through the carpet. She felt suddenly sick.

God, she hated this house now, she couldn't wait to leave. So many horrible memories. Every place that Michael had physically attacked her seemed to shout out at her. The dining table he liked to throw her over to abuse her. The stairs, which he had pushed her down when she had failed to iron the shirt he wanted to wear. The kitchen where he had scratched a noughts and crosses design on her upper arm with the tip of a sharp knife. She'd had to wear a long sleeved top for weeks, although it was summer, to give it a chance to heal. Upstairs didn't even bear thinking about. The bedroom: always trying not to cry or scream in case George heard her and came in.

Then the terrible fear that he would turn on George one day. She had seen signs of it starting to happen in the few months before he was murdered and it had terrified her.

The police had told her that the woman who killed Michael had got the wrong man. It turned out to be a case of mistaken identity. She was apparently seeking revenge on a man who had raped her daughter, the poor girl in the wheel-chair.

Who knew what lengths she herself would have gone to, if Michael had ever seriously hurt George. She shivered. It was a chilling thought. 'There but for the Grace of God go I…..'

She tried to clear her dark mood by getting up swiftly and moving some of the bags she'd left in the hall to one side, to make more room to get in and out. She must focus on the packing.

The phone rang and it was her Mum

'How are you doing, darling, do you need any help?'

'No thanks, Mum, I'm fine. Getting there, slowly,' Rachael said.

'Would you like me to have George for the day tomorrow as it's Saturday and there's no school?'

'Oh that would be such a help, Mum, if you're sure. What time shall I bring him over?'

'How about ten o'clock and I'll get Lorna to drop him back about five,' her mother said.

'Thanks so much, Mum,' said Rachael, looking at her watch. She had about an hour before she'd have to go and pick up George from school.

'Well I'll let you get on, darling,' her mother said and clicked off.

Rachael went into the kitchen and made herself a cup of tea. God she was tired, she'd have to sit down in a moment and take ten.

Her mother was coping really well since her father had died. Rachael had been worried she might fall to pieces, but she seemed to be made of sterner stuff and had surprised Rachael and Lorna with the way she'd handled everything. The dogs were proving to be a great help, a link with normality. She had to get them out every day and they were so loving and affectionate.

Lorna had been a support of course, by moving in with her for a bit. At least her mum hadn't had to cope with the strangeness of a silent empty house straight away, but now Lorna had a new boyfriend who she'd met at a Zumba class. He was divorced with a ten year old daughter and she was moving in with him next week.

Rachael had a sneaking suspicion that that her mum might be relieved and would enjoy having the house to herself now, to give her peace and quiet to reflect on her life with Dad, because when Lorna was living with you, life was all about Lorna, that was for sure.

She finished her tea and started filling a packing case with crockery, wrapping each plate in newspaper as she went.

An advertisement caught her eye.

'*Time to move on and put the past behind you*' it blared out, in large black letters.

Rachael smiled to herself.

'Too right,' she said, 'with you all the way.'

Chapter Sixty-five

It was the day of the move.

The child was half excited and half scared. He'd been running around all morning, watching the big burly men carrying things out of the house and loading them into an enormous van. The biggest he'd ever seen.

Mummy had taken him to look at their new home a few days ago and he liked it. They couldn't go in, as it was all locked up but they'd peeped through the front windows. You could see right through the house, and in the back garden was a shed like Grandad's. It was going to be his special place, he decided. Mummy had pointed to a window upstairs and said 'that's your room, George. It's bigger than the one you've got now, so there'll be lots of room for your lego. There was a tree with branches right outside his window. He'd be able to climb down it, easy-peasy, he thought.

Mummy said Duncan was going to come and live with them for a bit. The child quite liked the idea. He'd got used to him now and he was funny. He made Mummy laugh. He liked it when she laughed.

Another good thing was that the new place was near where Angus lived. They'd be able to walk round to each other's houses to play, whenever they wanted. And maybe even walk to school together on their own.

It felt strange watching his house get more and more empty. It didn't feel like their house at all any more. It looked different, like it was a pretend house.

When the last few bits had been taken out, Mummy said goodbye to the men and shut the front door.

She came and gave him a big hug.

'Come on darling, it's time to hop into the car and go to our new home! Isn't it exciting?'

'Are we ever coming back to this house, Mummy?' he asked.

'No, never,' she said, 'we don't need it any more. Someone else will come and live here now.'

'Just a minute, Mummy,' he said suddenly, and started for the stairs.

'Where are you going?' she asked.

'I want to say goodbye to my old room,' he said.

 Mummy laughed.

 'Go on then,' she said, 'I'll just get my bags from the kitchen.'

The child raced up the stairs to his bedroom. It looked huge with no bed or furniture and none of his toys.

He went over to the corner, bent down and carefully started

picking at the carpet, lifting it up. Yes, there it was. Grandad's special folding knife.

After he'd stolen it from Grandad's shed he hadn't known where to hide it. He knew he shouldn't have taken it but he really wanted to keep it. It was exciting and clever. He couldn't put it in with his toys, Mummy would find it and he'd get into trouble. He'd managed to prise up the corner of the carpet and slip it underneath. It was so thin you wouldn't even know it was there.

It was buried treasure. He could go and get it whenever he wanted it. Like when he and Angus had run away.

Sometimes he'd take it out, stroke the handle, open the blade and look at it, then quickly close it and put it back under the carpet. He'd put Mr Potts, his big monkey, leaning against the corner and you couldn't see it at all. He liked being the only person in the world who knew it was there.

Now he was leaving this house forever, he took it out for the last time and carefully opened it.

The sun coming through the window, shone on the silver blade and lit it up.

He looked at it for a moment, then snapped it shut and slipped it in his pocket.

A slow smile spread across his face.

Yes. He would use it properly one day.

Also by Pat Garwood

BEST WAY OUT

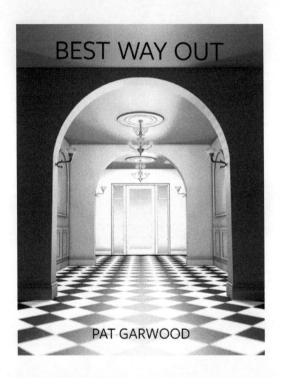

Best Way Out imagines a future where assisted death is a legal right for anyone over seventy-five. In South West London, Dr Alan Fordyke welcomes six guests who have chosen to end their days in style and comfort at Leeway Lodge, the clinic he has worked so hard to establish. Childhood memories, past loves and losses, triumphs and challenges, are interwoven into the events of their last evening. The tension is electric, as we approach the inevitable moment of truth, with anticipation, relief and even a sense of excitement. **Best Way Out** is a celebration of life, of age and experience, of racial and sexual diversity, and of a 'good' death.

It challenges us all to look at things a little differently.

BEST WAY OUT was published by Amanda Atkins in 2016 and is available in hardback, paperback or ebook from:

Lulu.com

Amazon

Barnes and Noble

Book Depository

WALNUTS

Walnuts

Who can resist temptation when it catches you unawares?

P a t   G a r w o o d

Walnuts is a modern-day tale of love and families set on the outskirts of London. It follows the day-to-day lives of the people who live in Princeton Road. We enter the thoughts of Eileen and Keith, who have just moved in to number 43 with their children; of old Mrs Anderson who lives in the upstairs flat at number 34 above Ian, who lives alone after his painful divorce. Jane and Tom and family are at number 51, and childless Penny and Michael complete the line up at number 40. We are drawn into their lives and dreams, as some find themselves caught up in extra-marital temptation; others deal with the death of loved ones; and we share the tender moments of a first sexual encounter. All this alongside the run up to an amateur production of 'Oh What a Lovely War'. We move from one character to another, learning their inner secrets as we see the world from their point of view, discovering their memories good and bad, and their current battles and triumphs. Within a few chapters it's as if we live in Princeton Road ourselves!

WALNUTS was published by Amanda Atkins in 2015 and is available in hardback, paperback or ebook from:

Lulu.com

Amazon

Barnes and Noble

Book Depository

KEYNE ISLAND

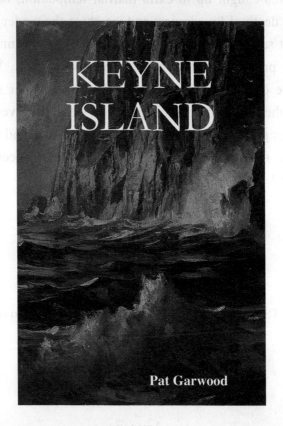

Keyne Island

ISLAND

Pat Garwood

Keyne Island is a passionate and original Victorian adventure. The plot twists and turns as it follows the fortunes and misfortunes of the Grundy family through three generations, exploring themes of love and money, greed and generosity, sexuality and family ties. Within a few pages, we are transported to a by-gone age and the rugged landscape of the small island intensifies the drama. With Clive, a heartless villain, at the centre of the story, and Mathew and young Dora bringing joy and optimism to this epic tale, good is pitched against evil with a moral integrity.

Although the book is set in the nineteenth century, it tackles contemporary themes, sensitively challenging our expectations of Victorian repression in its refreshing and open embracing of gay love. **Keyne Island** is an emotional rollercoaster, and the wild Cornish setting is so evocative you can almost smell the sea as you read.

KEYNE ISLAND was published by Amanda Atkins in 2014 and is available in hardback, paperback or ebook from:

Lulu.com

Amazon

Barnes and Noble

Book Depository"

www.patgarwood.com